KISS IN THE DARK

by
Mark Ellis

Note

The civilisations of Knossos and Mycenae flourished between 2100 and 1100 BC. Tiryns was built, and then destroyed by fire, towards the end of the Mycenean period. Ancient Tiryns and its ruins are a few miles away from Nafplion. The town was never on the sea, and there is no real modern Tiryns. However, in many ways the Tiryns of this book can indeed be found, lying almost at the head of the Bay of Argos. If there are degrees of difference, if there are alterations to the original, it is because this modern Tiryns is an imagined place, invented by each one of those who happens to visit it. Those who live there, throughout the year, know it by another name.

Greek names may have a variety of endings, such as Nicos, Nico, Nicou. For the sake of consistency, all names in this book have an 's' on the end.

KISS IN THE DARK is a work of fiction, and all the characters in its pages are imagined.

Efstathiadis Group S.A.
88, Drakontos Str., 104 42
Athens - GREECE

ISBN 960 226 562 0

© EFSTATHIADIS GROUP S.A. 1997

All rights reserved; no part of this
publication may be reproduced, stored in a
retrieval system or transmitted, in any form
or by any means, electronic, mechanical,
photocopying, recording, or otherwise, without the
prior permission of Efstathiadis Group S.A.

Printed and bound in Greece.

Acknowledgements

The author would like to acknowledge the very kind technical support given in the preparation of the manuscript by Richard Blaker. He would also like to thank Vivien Clark, Nathaniel Ellis and Printha Ellis for their detailed editing. Not least, he thanks warmly those large numbers of known and unknown, though witnessed, fellow human beings for their demonstrations of humanity, and their frequent acts of misbehaviour on the beach, which form the backdrop to this novel. Without them, nothing.

This book, a modern tragi-comedy in ten chapters, is dedicated to that wonderful spirit of tolerance on the part of the people of Greece which allows so many thousands of holidaymakers from the rest of the world to enjoy a few days of pleasure, each year, in that spectacular country.

About the author

Mark Ellis works as a training consultant in England. Previously, he has lived in North Africa, India and the Far East. Among his many publications there are several well-received novels, including *Bannerman* and *The Adoration of the Hanged Man,* published by Secker and Warburg. *Kiss In The Dark* was written over several summers in a popular taverna in the Tiryns of the book, and rewritten many times in Marlborough, England, where the author lives with his family.

About the book

What happens when a young British couple decide to drink every cocktail known at the head of the Bay of Argos? What happens when a woman alone decides to go for ice cream with a young man half her age? What happens when a chorus of beer swilling British hooligans arrive at the ancient theatre of Epidavros?

Kiss In The Dark is a cocktail of deceit, lies, sex and lack of sex, set on the beachfront of a popular Greek holiday resort. The book follows a group of holidaymakers on a two week package holiday and, like Mark Ellis' earlier novels, sets out to amuse and entertain. The various subplots deal with British and other foreign nationals abroad, and their entanglements with each other and the local culture. The story is seen partly through the eyes of the narrator, and partly through the narrative of one of the group, Julia Moore. Between them they relate details of beginnings and ends of relationships, gross misbehaviour, and even death. At the end, the holidaymakers go home, and the book itself can be left on the beach. The locals wait for the next group to appear, and the next chapter to be written.

What the critics have said

Bannerman

'Farcical fantastic novel with touch of comic genius' - *Books and Bookmen*

'*Bannerman* is one of the most powerful contemporary investigations into the recent accepted tyrannies of time and reason' - *Vogue*

'Dark, deep comedy' - Norman Shrapnel in *The Guardian*

Adoration of The Hanged Man

'Energetic and highly entertaining' - Jill Neville in *The Sunday Times*

'Hilarious'- Nina Bawden in *The Daily Telegraph*

ONE

Maeve has sat for most afternoons of the week in the outside bar of the Delphi Hotel, staring at the nearby island of Romvi, and in particular at the two large hills which have given the island its more popular name, Aphrodite. The sea between the mainland and the island, and its smaller sister island, Coronisi, is narrow - only a few hundred metres at most - but there are times of the day when the current runs fast, and the wind blows the waves across the surface in strong swells. For much of the day, however, the water and the sea further to the west and south of the town of Tiryns is covered by a variety of small craft - pedallos, fishing vessels, catamarans, power boats, and from time to time larger ocean-going yachts.

Maeve's afternoon vigils are broken only by cups of coffee, brought out by Maria, the teenage sister of the hotel manager, Alexos. Maeve herself does not go unnoticed.

The guests at the hotel are quick to register the woman who regularly sits alone in the afternoon, a paperback and sometimes a notepad on her table, and who seems to stare out for such long intense periods at the sea, the small boats, the swimmers, and the islands. She wishes to be alone. No one approaches her. The occasional smile, the occasional indications that someone might be about to join her, lead to sudden movement on her part, a hand inside a large wicker beach bag, a gesture to Maria to bring more coffee, and even on one afternoon a rush for the door leading to the ladies' room. The only person she appears to allow near her is Maria, and from time to time, given that his attentions are often devoted to other aspects of managing the largest and oldest hotel in Tiryns, Alexos himself.

Maria works during the summer on the beach, but for most of the year she is in Athens, studying languages. She is slight and wears loose fitting blouses and long black shorts. Her cheeks are hollow, but her eyes are quick. She follows the tourists intently, and she listens for words to respond to, and laughs loudly when her own response causes interest or pleasure.

'Efharisto, Maria.' Maeve acknowledges the arrival of her third coffee of the afternoon.

'Working again?' Maria's eyes are black, and deep, and they light up briefly, suggesting that her question might be a reprimand.

'Yes, again.' Maeve smiles back at Maria and feels, with unexpected curiosity, that the eyes of this young Greek woman are familiar. They remind her of her own.

Maeve is sallow skinned and tall. Her long black hair is thick and expressive; it is rarely unnoticed. As Maeve Philips she has a public image which no one on this beach is aware of. She has sunk into this week of privacy, sunk into these rare hours of silence and liberty; she has spent hours alone on the beach in the early morning and listened to herself breathing.

'Why Greece?' Martin had asked her. She remembers him staring at her and the sullen question, almost an accusation. 'Why Greece?' Martin's persistence is part of something else. It is a danger to that weak underside of her own private world, that edge of privacy which borders on isolation, which calls up shadows, which has horizons that often come far too close, bearing down on her. At night she dreams heavily, and often her dreams are nightmares. 'Why Greece?' she had retaliated. 'I should have thought you might have been interested. Is it part of Europe or isn't it? Is it in the present or is it in the past? That sort of thing. Right up your street.'

That had been several weeks ago, in London.

Maria walks away, and Maeve is caught by the girl's legs. They are long and brown, and the skin is smooth, glowing like warm polished wood. Maeve catches herself drifting back to her husband, Martin. Tomorrow, Saturday morning, her own relationship with this place, the beach, the people, will have to change. Martin will bring his own concerns, his own carefully selected instruments of measurement. Of course, the truth is that Martin had been jealous of her coming here on her own. Europe is Martin's scene, not hers. He is the great European, the great intercultural expert, and her coming alone to Greece like this has challenged his authority. Maeve's eyes light up. She had always thought that Martin's so-called profession as a trainer to the great corporations of the world was so much hot air.

Out on the beach, Spyros, a gynaecologist from Athens, stands talking to Christos, whose pedallo business this year is paying for his sister's education in Athens. Nodding towards Maeve, Christos says, 'She looks Greek.' 'Maybe,' Spyros replies thoughtfully, ' but she is English. She puts milk in her coffee and she bought her swimming costume at Marks and Spencer. I know. She took her top off to go in the water and I looked at the label.'

Georgios' cat lies still at the foot of the rough concrete wall that separates the patio of the Hotel Delphi from the beach. The cat is old and will in a matter of hours be dead. Georgios waits impatiently for it to die. The animal's thin and mangy body and the painful tortured nightly wandering among the tables of his taverna have begun to cause comment among the tourists, even among the more regular guests.

Like most of the hotels and small converted fishermen's cottages that lie just metres back from the beach, the Hotel Delphi this August is busy. Now, it is already nearly midnight but several of the tables still bear small bottles of retsina, half empty carafes of ouzo, and heavily used ashtrays. Small groups of Greeks, French and Italians raise voices above the alternating sounds of Cliff Richard and Roy Orbison coming from a huge pair of loudspeakers set to the far right of the hotel patio. The night itself is still. There is a large dusty tree in the middle of the patio, and its leaves do not move. The beat of the music travels through the concrete slabs of the patio floor and out through the wall, to where the black and white cat lies stretched out on dried leaves. A crushed milk carton and an old, stained plastic bag lie under its body and rear legs. After a while, as though revived by the music, it lurches to its feet and slowly staggers down the beach towards Georgios' taverna.

Like the night the sea is still, here and there

reflecting the harsh light from the lamps the mayor has chosen to have placed at irregular intervals along the waterfront. One of these silver reflections diverts the animal from its progress down the beach, and it stops just short of the water's edge. A woman approaches. The cat is aware of her but does not turn its head. The water ripples, and with it the light.

Maeve has had dinner with Luigi, an elderly Italian from Turin, whose knowledge of Tiryns goes back over thirty years. He is a permanent member of the town's summer population, driving across from Italy in late July and leaving again in the early days of September. He sits back in his chair and as always has dressed very carefully, his brown trousers pressed, his white shirt fresh and selected for the evening, even though only spent humbly and frugally over a plate of fresh fish and a bottle of white wine.

Luigi is known for his smile, which he dispenses regularly, and for his quick humour. His English is flavoured with zest, and he uses it to bring ease and laughter among strangers. 'So,' he says to Maeve, 'tonight your husband is coming to Athens.' He shakes his head; the gesture says it all. The concrete. The pollution. The dust. A lone fly crawls across the table. Luigi snaps at it with his right hand and captures it in Maeve's upturned metaxa glass. 'In August,' he pronounces, 'there seem to be few flies. Look here. Just one. But in September there are thousands. Flies everywhere.' 'And why is that?' Maeve asks, unaware of the trap. The Italian leans forward and whispers, 'Because in August there are thousands of tourists. Tourists everywhere. Here, and down there.' He points to the other end of the beach. 'And so, for each tourist there is maybe only one fly. But in September the tourists are only a few.' He shrugs his shoulders. The logic of the argument is irrefutable. 'And so, for each tourist there are many more flies.' He shrugs his shoulders again, grins, and leans back in his chair.

When Maeve gets up to leave Luigi half rises and says goodnight. He tells her he has enjoyed meeting her. She runs. 'Oh, Tiryns,' she says to herself, whispering magic as her feet fly across the sand. She has read of trance walkers in Tibet, and seen them in her dreams, moving swiftly across strange mountainous horizons, but now it is more likely to be the metaxa, she reasons. She sees a red moon, a half disc, rising slowly above the island of Coronisi, then comes to a stop as an old and tired black and white cat in front of her stares as if mesmerised at the light in the water. 'Oh, Tiryns,' she repeats. The cat moves slowly away, up towards the concrete wall at the head of the beach.

And time appears to stop.

'I have been watching you for such a long time,' the voice says. It comes from behind her, but she doesn't turn. She is sitting at a table, one of several placed in front of a taverna. The moon is higher now. Georgios' cat, unknown to her, lies only a few metres away, waiting for the moon to disappear, for the day to come.

And then she turns her head, and sees Spyros, the gynaecologist, sitting behind her at the next table. 'Believe me,' he says, 'I have seen a lot of very beautiful women.'

'You have?' she queries, telling herself at the same time she should have ignored the man. He grins, and she wonders how she has got herself into this situation. 'Yes, believe me.' Spyros is thirty two years old. His wife is a model. He has a new BMW parked outside The Delphi, which he intends to drive back to Athens at seven in the morning, but meanwhile he is here on the beach with this woman. Maeve sees eyes which look at her earnestly, and she registers the great shock of black hair, and the unexpectedly delicate fingers.

'I think I've had too much metaxa,' she says.

'And I should go to bed.'

'I think you are extraordinarily beautiful. You mustn't worry about the metaxa. You're on holiday. You're here to play, to do nice things.'

'Actually, I wish you wouldn't say that. I don't even know you.'

'I'm sorry, but it would have been a crime not to say it. Excuse me, I don't wish to embarrass you.' His fingers touch her arm, and she registers the authority.

'I must go,' she says. She looks around, ready to get up.

'Takis!' Spyros signals quickly, and a young boy approaches out of the shadows.
'Two espressos.' The boy acknowledges and disappears. 'Please. I want you to have the best coffee in Greece. And then,' he smiles, 'I will say goodnight.' Maeve is nearly ten years older than Spyros. She stares past him, and sees movement in the shadows as the young boy brings them coffee. 'He is my cousin,' Spyros enlarges, raising both hands up to the level of the table top. Delicate fingers play with the handle of the cup, daring her to look, but she turns her gaze to the slight figure of the boy, the nonchalance, the ease in his lack of movement as he stands there watching. The boy is no more than twelve or thirteen years old. And this other one, the man? She plays with her coffee

spoon. 'My husband comes tomorrow,' she tells him.

'That's nice.' The man smiles encouragingly at her.

'Why are you trying to make love to me?' she asks. He leans across the gap. 'You are a beautiful woman. I'd be crazy not to.' She looks for the slightest evidence of repentance in the announcement, but finds none. Of course, he knows what she is thinking, and the smile never leaves his face. 'You know, this doesn't happen in England,' she tells him.

Spyros nods. 'When I go to England I go to see the museums. Or maybe the shops.' They finish their coffee, and he reaches for her arm. 'I'll take you back, like I promised. Up there, to The Delphi.'

'You know my hotel?'

'Of course.'

When they arrive he does not relent. 'Shall I come inside? Alexos is my cousin.'
And quite without knowing why she turns and faces this stranger outside the hotel entrance, with the great breasts of Aphrodite behind her and the half disc of the moon riding high above, and says, 'I haven't slept with a man for months.'

Spyros is genuinely shocked and recoils. 'Not even your husband?'

Maeve shakes her head, and her hair flows across her cheeks as she says, 'Not even my husband.'

'The man must be crazy,' the Greek mutters. Maeve goes inside and hears him call after her, but she goes on, and leaves him. Spyros is left alone. Behind him a fishing boat moves out of the harbour. It is Kostas, Dimitris' brother. Dimitris, the owner of The Ship, one of the better known bars in Tiryns, whose lights Spyros can see three hundred metres down the beach.

Alexos joins him, and the two men stand just a few centimetres from the edge of the water, watching it twist and swing the light that comes down from above Coronisi, and leave it in small surging dark ripples that bubble finally into the sand.

In the hotel behind, Maeve stands on her balcony and watches the two men.

Late again. Always late. Stavros greets the appearance of the bus from Athens by draining the large cup of black coffee which on this and every morning represents his breakfast. The road winds along the cliff top and the windows of the bus throw flashes of sunlight back across the bay. Stavros narrows his eyes and listens, then smiles as he catches the familiar straining in the gears as Vangelis swings through the corners. 'Damn lousy driver,' he says aloud in English, though no one but an old ginger cat stretched out in the shadows beneath the hibiscus is there to hear him. Even at this distance Stavros is aware of the silence when the bus stops suddenly, hidden in a grey pool of shadow by the villa that old Georgios finished the previous summer. He reaches for the binoculars next to the now empty coffee cup and searches in the shadows by the villa.

There is a crumpled square of paper in his pocket which he has picked up from the office earlier in the week. Like a dozen others in his care, all equally crumpled, it is a fax. No, he'd told his brother, Andreas, he hadn't taken it. What would he want with a fax meant for someone else? He pulls out the fax and focuses on it. 'Family Bullock. Two adults. One son. One daughter. Two weeks Villa Georgios. August 10th. Return Gatwick September 2nd.'

A wasp drifts over the wooden balcony rail, and vanishes through the open shutters of the house. Stavros stares after it, then once again lifts the binoculars. He catches movement, and spots Louise, the courier who works for Andreas. Next, a man's face, bearing a large moustache, appears from the left. Then Louise again, mounting the bus. He lingers over her legs as she disappears inside. Lowering the binoculars he screws up his eyes and stares across the few hundred metres of blue water, and the still morning air above it, that separate his small villa, white and blue on the cliff edge, and the bus from the airport that only now moves out from its pool of shadow. But Louise is Yannis' girl, and last year Yannis had head-butted him to the ground at the suggestion that her favours could be had quite freely, given the right combination of beer, ouzo, and time of night. Well, the truth is maybe he does like Louise, but Yannis has a foul temper and a reputation as a head-butter, and as far as he, Stavros, is concerned, Yannis can keep the bitch.

The bus goes round by Assini, ancient Assini. Stavros looks at the familiar old rocks, and the water beneath them, but his imagination shows him no triremes, no temples, no ancient forefathers. Instead, it resurrects more recent images - Julia from Warwick, Jodie from Durham, Deborah from Scotland, another Julia from somewhere in Wales and the small blonde from that place near London, and her friend he'd had on a Friday night while the little blonde was throwing up on the beach. The bus disappears, but he knows where it is - hidden by the olive trees on the far side of Assini, where he'd found the blonde from Finland lying stark naked in the middle of the day, protected from the ants and the sharp stones by a rush mat. 'I've never been to Finland,' he'd said, eyeing all of her. 'What's it like?' She'd got up, flicked the mat, and walked off. 'Cold,' he thought she'd said. But he hadn't been sure.

He doesn't understand half of what the girls say, unlike Michaelis, the pharmacist, who understands everything - English, French, German, Swedish. Stavros leans over the balcony and spits. He watches the spittle spread into droplets as it falls towards the rocks nearly seventy metres below. Michaelis is a smartass. He laughs at his memories of Michaelis. So many of them. There he is, the pharmacist, the proud educated son of his father, and yet the previous year he was the only one to have caught anything. From that German woman who'd hounded him up and down the main street for two weeks in June, a large woman of great purpose, who came from Lubeck, and whose husband had died of a heart attack on a pedallo the year before. So, Michaelis had got the clap, while he, Stavros, is an impregnable fortress, boosted by monstrous doses of vitamin C, honey and yogurt, taken three times daily in the season. He'd told the secret to Michaelis, perhaps unwisely giving him the formula which for the past ten years had kept him so vigorous and uninfected, but

Michaelis had laughed, and then got gonorrhoea.

Ten o'clock. The town of Tiryns, at the head of the bay of Argos, wakes to another day of heat. The cats know it and hide. One of them, old Georgios' black and white cat, quietly crawls into a scrap of shade in the broken concrete and brickwork under the verandah of the Villa Diana, and waits to die.

The horn blasts as the bus comes down the road from Assini, and Stavros trains the binoculars on it as it swings into the new town. He holds it steady for seconds as it moves past the ten year old skeleton of the unfinished Plaza Hotel, then loses it for good. But he knows the route, and across the still water, and through the rising heat, he tracks it past The Apollo and into the old town. Past The Ship, and fat Spyros' bar, the London Pub, the Post Office and the Artemis Hotel, white and blue, covered in bougainvillea. Stavros has pulled the other faxes from his pocket. Family Porter. Family Graham. Mr Jones and Mrs Hillier. Where are the faxes? Andreas had asked, and he had stared straight back at Andreas and said that he knew nothing about the faxes. He wasn't even part of the business. How could he know about the faxes?

He tears the faxes to shreds, one by one, and they float slowly from his hand, over the balcony and down. Stavros stares after the bits of paper as they float down to the rocks and the sea that spills over them. So much goes over the balcony. Each day.

There is one fax left. 'Family Moore. Julia and George Moore. Daughter, Gail, aged 15. One boy. Villa Diana.' Stavros closes his eyes and conjures up a young girl, very pale, slowly walking across the few metres of beach outside the Villa Diana, and placing her foot tentatively in the water. He takes in breath quickly. Gail Moore. No one has instinct like his, no one, not even his brother, with all his success and his money. Andreas can go to hell, and his damned travel agency with him. Stavros curses Minoa Travel, and imagines Andreas falling over the balcony, down to the rocks and the sea below.

Music brings him round quickly, and he focuses his attention on a brightly flagged fishing boat only a few hundred metres away. Kostas. Now there is a fine fat man. Stavros watches him come in towards the small port of Tiryns, laden with octopus. The sound of the bouzouki heightens, and drifts up, as if just for him. Stavros waves. In the small cabin on the vessel a balding, burnt-faced man, belly blown with years of beer on winter evenings huddled over cards at Yannis' place, catches the movement on Stavros' balcony and sounds the horn. It echoes across the bay. 'The most beautiful bay on earth', Andreas had written in his brochure, Stavros remembers. Or was it written by that sick young man who had come from London? 'Tiryns, a white pearl, set at the head of the most beautiful bay on earth, faced by islands, protected by the massive hills behind.'

'The hills are not massive,' Stavros had pointed out quite reasonably to his brother. 'And they smell of shit from May to September.' Stavros looks across the bay again, revelling in the familiar, the small island, Coronisi, and the big island, Aphrodite, with her two breasts rising proud in the centre. And then the others, further south in the bay towards Spetses.

'It's for the photographs.' Andreas had been philosophical in his explanation. 'Photographs don't smell.'

The heat rises. The pedallos come out. Over by the harbour Dimitris' younger brother, Christos, is out with the power boat. Once again Stavros spits over the balcony. Time to go into town.

'Mum. Mum.'
Julia Moore wrinkles her nose on the balcony of

the Villa Diana. 'Her' balcony. She pats the rail, and the red and blue striped towel already wet from the first swim. 'The first swim.' She relishes the words, and turns them over and and over, and looks across the sea to Aphrodite. Did they really look like breasts, those bare yet bristling hills? Did they?

'Mum, you didn't bring the factor eight.' The complaint comes from the flat above her. Julia stands still and listens. 'Yes, I did.' The woman's reply is quiet and reasonable.

'No, you didn't,' the boy replies. Only the factor four, and that's bloody useless.'

Julia leans on the railing, against the wet towel and looks up towards the offending conversation above. Factor eight? She wonders what they are arguing about. Her attention moves back to the movement of pedallos on the water and the mixed undercurrent of Greek, German, English and French that flows along the beach below her.

'Yes, you did say you'd packed the factor eight. You did.' Julia hears the boy's voice, sharp and accusing.

'I don't use factor eight.'

'But I do.'

'I had other things to think about,' the woman's voice replies patiently.

Once again Julia looks upwards. She thinks she

knows them, and tries to remember, but she is
tired, and all those people, the flight, that awful
journey from Athens. She can't think. She coughs,
dismissing the family above her, touches her neck
with one hand, and gazes towards the sea in front,
the old outcrop of ruined Assini to the left, and
Aphrodite with those two old hills to the right, and
in front of her the pedallos. At the edge of the
water a woman stands alone. Julia watches her
slowly dipping her hand into the sea and pouring
water over shoulders. 'Oh, Tiryns,' she says to
herself, and half closes her eyes. She repeats the
words. 'Oh, Tiryns.'

Julia sits in the small patch of shade under her red
beach umbrella, her knees drawn up, her hands
clasped around them. Seen from a short distance
away, from the shade of the next umbrella, whose
elderly and portly owner has now at this instant
just returned from the water, Julia appears tense.
In fact, she isn't. Her thin and neat body, her
sharply angled face, her carefully cropped hair, are
part of a system she likes to think of as well-tuned,
but which friends and relations, and her husband,
George, often think of as tense, nervous, tightly
drawn. 'No, I am not feeling tense, George. I am
fine. I am on holiday and I feel absolutely

wonderful.' That had only been an hour ago, as George had collapsed onto the bed in the villa.

'I am not tense,' she had repeated.

'Suit yourself.'

Julia tells herself that this is her first holiday for ten years and she is going to enjoy herself, and George and the children and everybody else had better not get in her way.

She spreads her toes in the sand and thinks of George asleep on the bed. The sand burns and she lets out a quick yelp.

On the flight out there had been a Mrs Simmons, who had questioned her about what her husband did for a living. 'He teaches.' Julia's reply had been swift and to the point. 'Ah, and do you do that, too?' The question was accompanied by a long, searching look.

'No, I don't.' This time the reply had been curt. She noticed that Mrs Simmons was thin, with vulture brown skin on her neck and face.

'Ah, so it's only your husband who teaches.'

'Yes, he's a sort of headmaster.'

'Oh, Good Heavens!' Mrs Simmons had said, and the shadow of a companion called Betty had sucked her teeth and said 'Good Heavens!' too, before adding, 'What a responsibility!'

Julia reminds herself to be wary of Mrs Simmons and her companion. Now, she looks with proud ownership across the bay, at the islands, the pedallos, the power boat swinging a water skier in a wide parabola, and the disconnected heads and arms of the swimmers moving between the motorboats and dinghies anchored just off the shoreline. Of course, the truth is she could have been a teacher. She ventures a toe forward again into the sand, then pulls back. Beware the heat, she is reminded. In England the radio had told them of people dying in Athens.

'Greece? No, darling. Turkey this year. Greece is so, well, never mind. Anyway, have fun. I've heard Tiryns is different.' Julia searches for the face behind that voice, and finds it. George's sister, Rachel.

Now, on the beach, Julia's eyes focus, fix and harden. Light blue. 'The strangest and palest blue,' had always been the comment. 'By far the best thing in a very ordinary face,' she'd overheard George's mother confiding to a friend. Julia sniffs. George's mother is dead. The truth, of course, is that she ought to have qualified too, got diplomas and certificates and the rest, but they were young and only one of them could go cn to college; and, of course, she got pregnant. Which is why, inexorably, she isn't a teacher and works instead for that creep of a solicitor at Dixon and Brown. The unwelcome image of Lawrence Brown's face taunts her, and it is only with an effort that she chases it away. She should feel tired, of course. That bloody awful flight, not that she is going to admit that it had been awful. Ever. Let George do the complaining.

And George sleeps, on that, well, not so very pleasant bed. Thin, very spare sheets, and that hard mattress. Rachel would have had a word to say, but then Rachel is in a hotel in Turkey, and frankly Rachel can stuff herself. Julia is surprised at her own vulgarity. She looks up quickly, to the right along the beaches, and then moves her lips just so, in a manner that once nights and nights and years and years ago, George had called pensive. George has not aged well. He is only thirty seven, but old. She digs in the sand with her fingers, and lets the grains slip and fall. Of course, other women sometimes met men. Last year, it had been Mary. Mary had met someone. She hadn't said much, except that he'd been older. But Julia doesn't trust her. No, Mary had met a younger man.

In front of her a lone swimmer comes in towards the shore. It is Stavros. Julia watches the water run off him, the droplets falling from his black ringlets, the sheen on those small briefs around his hips. It takes a while before she realises what she is doing, that she is watching him.

He approaches and passes.

Of course, George has a white paunch. There are folds, not only in the front, but at the sides. George is passing visibly into middle age. Julia lies back, and stretches her legs apart. It's hot. She closes her eyes. And suddenly, she's tired.

Julia wakes, throwing herself up frantically into a sitting position. The sun blinds her, and her face and shoulders burn. 'Tom!' Her son's name is hardly uttered. It is more of a lightly phrased question. Where in the hell is he, anyway? She lurches to her feet and walks gingerly across the few yards of white hot sand. Reaching the villa she calls out to her husband. 'George?' Her watch tells her it is two o'clock in the afternoon; her body tells her to go back to sleep. Like George, lying diagonally across the bed, mouth half open. She stands, one knee against the bed, watching him. The patchy red face, large nose, large hands, large ears, large feet.

'George!' He hears her, she knows that. A light ripple moves across his face. 'George. Where is Tom?'

'God knows.' He manages the two words, then turns, first to the left, then to the right. She stares at the sparse black hair creeping over the top of his vest. That vest. A large tear from a yellow stain under the right armpit reaches towards the waist.

Hadn't she thrown it away two or three weeks ago? Of course she had, and that dirty bastard must have retrieved it from the rubbish. 'For God's sake, we've only been here four hours and the kids have disappeared. I told you this would happen.' George opens one eye and fights back. 'No, you didn't. I told you it would happen.' She starts to reply, but George is clever and has succumbed yet again to sleep.

Julia stands at the foot of the bed, a slight figure, whose short fine hair has picked up a net of dry sand. The fingers of her right hand splay out, then draw in. 'They're your children, George Moore,' she enunciates slowly. He knows it, and sleeps on.

Back on the beach Julia watches a young man slowly pour a stream of white lotion on the shoulders of a woman who, Julia thinks, well, could be his mother. His mother, lover, turns and smiles hullo. An ordinary forgettable face. God, how could she? Must be twice his age. And what would he be, then? Twenty two? Twenty five, at most?

'Oh, Christ!' A man's voice explodes just a few metres away. She recognises him from the plane. A paunchy, red-faced man with a moustache. And there was a wife, and two children. 'Who in the hell let them out?' There is no doubt who he is referring to. He and Julia, and the young man with the older woman, sit together in an arc, teamed together, faces turned to their right, their attention focused on a group of three young men.

'Louts,' says the man with the moustache. He grins hurriedly at Julia, she at him, and they nod at the same time, acknowledging that they belong together, had shared that awful flight, now share this beach, these islands, and share revulsion of these three young men, tattooed, pale skinned, who stand just a few metres away, a can of beer held firmly in each right hand.

Julia instinctively feels that she should be more generous - why should they be louts? She is not a prejudiced woman. George, of course, has his prejudices. Well, he does. And so, obviously, does the man with the moustache. But she prides herself on her lack of prejudice. However, she can't resist staring at them. And realising that she is doing so she smiles. They are perhaps twenty years old. All wear long Bermuda shorts. All are bare chested. All wear ear-rings. All have close cropped hair. The man with the moustache leans towards Julia. 'I'm, Jo,' he says. 'Bullock. I remember you and your family.' He pauses, then adds enigmatically, 'Tired? Asleep? Mine is.'

Statements and questions rattle together. 'Oh, yes,' Julia says. 'Yes. I'm Julia. Moore. George is asleep.'

'Fuck Greece.'

Julia coughs and Jo Bullock shakes his head. The two determine not to recognise the source of the comment.

'Fuck Greece.'

'Awful journey, wasn't it?' Julia says quickly.

'Yes, awful. Diabolical, really.'

One of the three men is taller than the others, and his face is long and horselike. His arms are thin, and his chest and body so empty that Julia wonders if he ever eats. 'I've seen the cat,' he pronounces. It is a proclamation. A declaration of achievement. The three of them raise their cans and drink. The first to finish turns quickly seawards and hurls the can in a high arc upwards. As it spins upwards the thrower loses balance and lurches to the left, knocking into a companion. Both fall, and rise again seconds later, laughing hysterically. 'I've seen the cat,' the tall one says again.

'You're fucking mad.'

'It's got flies.'

'Flies? You've got flies on your fucking brain.'

Julia watches as the tall one is pulled down into the water. Jo Bullock rubs the sand off his hands.

'I was rather hoping there wouldn't be any of them here,' he says apologetically.

'Must have missed the plane to Ibiza,' says the young man behind them.

'Can't understand how we can let them out of the country,' Jo adds.

'I suppose they've got to go somewhere,' the older woman says reasonably.

Julia wonders about that, then wonders why she is wondering, and is suddenly angry that here, on this first day of holiday, she is sitting on a beach with a group of people from her own country, making comments about nothing other than some of their fellow holidaymakers. 'I hope they don't spoil it,' a single voice rings out. It is only later that Julia realises that the voice was her own.

As the young men move away, throwing water at each other and yelling, she wonders about the cat. What cat?

'I've never been to Greece before,' says the older woman. The declaration, invitation, goes unanswered. Her young partner continues to rub oil into her back, slowly. Unobserved, Julia watches.

'Betty. Betty.' Mrs Simmons' voice rises sharply as she taps Betty's shoulder. Terrible thing Betty's wearing. Probably Marks and Spencer. Betty turns to her, her eyes wide, her mouth open in that silly grin she always adopts when suddenly summoned. 'Betty, I wish you wouldn't always grin like that.'

'Well, I don't mean to, Harriet. You know that.'

The two women are regulars at The Delphi. For Andreas at Minoa Travel they have a special significance because they were in the very first group that he brought out to Tiryns at the end of the seventies. For Alexos, the manager of the hotel, they also bring back memories, each time he sees them - the same faces, the same strange clothes, the same binoculars. And it is the binoculars he and many others in Tiryns remember them for most. Every summer it is the same, with Betty sitting next to Harriet Simmons on the large patio of the hotel, sweeping the beach and the sea in front of them with those binoculars, a Leica Harriet's father had brought back from Germany, just before the Second World War.

'Over there!' Harriet says urgently. 'There! What is it?'

Betty focuses on a small group of people a little way down the beach. She sees two women and a man.

'Well?'

Betty struggles with the binoculars. Her eyes

are going. Each year the evidence becomes stronger. 'It's a man and two women,' she pronounces finally.

'Good grief, woman, even I can see that. But what are those other things?'

Betty shifts her attention to what appear to be a large plastic whale and an enormous plastic armchair. She lowers the binoculars in disbelief and shakes her head. Apart from a young barman from Athens the two women are alone on the hotel patio of The Delphi, to their mind the best hotel at this, the 'British' end of the beach. The British end is what Harriet Simmons always calls it, Betty remembers, in recognition of the way the French and the Swiss and the Germans tend to stay at the other end in the new hotels and camping sites, nearly two kilometres away round the point. Betty stares keenly at the small white haired woman who for the past ten years has been her sole defence against the realities of the outside world. Provider of family, house, and money.

The small group of three come closer and eventually stop just a few metres away in front of the hotel. Harriet and Betty stare at the large plastic whale and the equally large plastic blow-up armchair, each one secured by one of the women. The man, short, very muscular, middle aged, stands to one side, one hand gently but persistently scratching the back of his thigh. 'They're Germans, aren't they?' Harriet says firmly.

'Oh, I don't think they're Germans, Harriet. The Germans go the other end. They always have done. Ever since we've been coming here.'

'Then why are they speaking German, Betty? Really, woman, you speak such nonsense.'

'They're Austrian,' Betty pronounces firmly, surprising herself with the enormity of the initiative.

'Oh, Good Heavens!' Harriet says, ignoring the reply and walking quickly across to the side of the patio. She is in time to see the man in the water make a sudden rush at the whale, which has cleverly slipped to one side so that the headlong lunge misses completely. His two companions stand their ground, their ample bodies strapped into flowered one-piece swim suits, their hair equally wrapped away. As the man comes up for air, they laugh and shout words of encouragement, which lead the man to turn and face the whale again. Yet another demonic rush through the water precedes a flying leap through the air, which this time takes the man slithering onto the whale's back. For a second he holds tight, secured in part by the two women who are fastened to its head, but the moment is short lived and seconds later the whale rolls belly up and smothers its rider in a cascade of spume.

'My God!' Harriet Simmons exclaims in astonishment. Betty feels her companion's hand reach for her arm, and tighten. As the man reappears from the water, shakes his head and snorts angrily through his cupped hands, he is greeted by words of advice from the two women. On the hotel patio a small crowd gathers. They observe that the man appears to distrust the whale, and turns his attention to the vast but more benign proportions of the armchair, which bobs up and down, empty and aloof on the water. The man rubs his hands and saunters up to the chair. He pushes it. It floats off. He follows it. His progress is followed by whispered encouragement in German. He reaches out again, but this time the pursuing hands are followed by a mighty thrusting of body and a great shout. The man mounts the chair, his face glows, but only seconds later he is dethroned as the entire edifice capsizes. But the would-be king and rider nonetheless impresses his small audience with his persistence. Emerging from the water, he gathers the two women in his embrace. He harnesses them to the chair, echoing his directions with gestures. His hands point and the women seize the chair and hold it steady. He mounts from the front, and sits down.

Mounted in the chair, the man is helpless. He

straddles it, backside buried in air and plastic, short legs hanging over the front, short arms carving the air over the sides, swirling like windmills as they desperately reach down towards the water, where on a happier body they would more effectively operate as paddles. It is not to be. The huge plastic chair drifts out to sea, spinning slowly round in the water as the wind comes in from the bay beyond Aphrodite. The women shout instructions. The man's arms swirl around pathetically in reply.

'Good God, how vulgar,' Harriet Simmons chokes, laughing. 'Such a thoroughly stupid man. A typical German.'

'He's probably a bank manager,' Betty ventures.

'Don't be silly, Betty. He's a lorry driver. Something like that. Anyway, I wish they'd stay at their end of the beach.' Betty is pulled away. As she leaves, she notices one of the women pulling the discarded whale down the beach. There is a message written in bright red letters down its side, which she can just make out as saying 'BANK. SALZBURG.'

'Where's Salzburg, Harriet?' Betty asks cheerfully. 'Isn't it in Germany?'

'Of course not. Salzburg is in Austria,' the answer is snapped back. Betty grins, and sighs, and is happy. As they walk back to the lift she finds her arm pulled sharply, and Harriet facing her. 'Why?'

Harriet asks her. 'Why did you ask me about Salzburg?'

'Oh, nothing, Harriet. Nothing, really. Just curious.'

'Tom!'

Julia Moore rushes up the beach towards the villa. Damn the boy, and damn George. If George would only take his responsibilities more seriously, then Tom wouldn't be so difficult. Her arms swing out at her sides as she comes to the steps. But before going further she is alerted by a familiar yet strangely unexpected form lying in the shadows of the wall at the base of the villa. Gingerly, she goes towards it. The villa stands on a concrete platform above the beach, but over the years the concrete has eroded in places, leaving cavernous holes which tourists and locals alike treat as a deposit for discarded bottles, cans and other rubbish.

It is a cat which, though not dead, is obviously not far short of it. 'Ugh!' Julia jumps back. 'George!.' She runs into the villa and finds her husband sitting on the edge of the bed.

'Have you seen my camera?' he asks her.

'Camera? No. Where's Tom?'

'Tom?'

'Yes, our child. Where is he?'

'With you, isn't he?'

'And George, you've got to get rid of the cat. I am not staying in this place with that thing lying out there. It's covered in flies.'

'What cat?'

'The one outside, in the hole. It's dead, or dying, and I won't stay here unless you do something about it.'

'Christ, what do you want me to do? Give it the kiss of life?'

'Don't be ridiculous. That is not what I said and you know it is not what I meant.'

'Alright, alright,' George says, preparing to shift tack again. 'Anyway, where's my camera? Are you sure you didn't put it in your bag?'

'I do not believe this. Tom is missing and all you can talk about is your camera. You've got to find him.'

'I thought you were worried about the cat.'

'No, I am worried about Tom. The cat is something else.'

'Tom'll turn up.'

'No!' She stands in front of him, and taking her in quickly, the pointing finger, the feet planted firmly, the thrust of her chin, he knows she is furious.

'OK, I'll talk to someone about the cat.'

'Who? And find Tom!' Julia drops onto the

bed, exhausted. 'I'm tired.'

'You should get some sleep.'

'Where do you think he is?'

'With Gail,' George suggests.

'He's never with Gail. Don't be ridiculous.'

George opens the top drawer of the old and scarred chest of drawers that their room is provided with, and pulls out a pair of binoculars. 'There's loads of English here,' she says. 'I met some of them.' George goes across to the windows and opens the shutters. 'Nice?' he asks.

'A fattish man with a moustache.'

'Oh, yes.' George scans the water.

'What are you doing?' she asks.

'Looking for Tom. Maybe he's on one of those things. Pedallos.'

'He doesn't have any money,' she counters.

'He always has money.'

'And there was a toyboy,' she continues, remembering the beach. 'A woman and a younger man. Loads younger. Quite, I don't know, quaint.'

'Quaint?'

'Yes. Imagine, well, you know, with someone half your age.'

'There are some very nice twenty year old men around, Julia.' Sweeping the bay George finds nothing, except for a young woman on a pedallo, her face hidden by her long hair, sitting next to a man. The man has his arm round her. The woman's breasts ride high and George dwells on them.

'What can you see?'

'Nothing.'

'George?' Julia says after a while. 'Are we going to enjoy this holiday?'

'Yes.'

'Do you want to?'

'Yes. Of course. What kind of question is that?' He holds the binoculars steady. The woman's hair blows tantalizingly across her face, her breasts; the man reaches out and runs his fingers through the hair, and down.

George lets the binoculars drop, and his eyes widen.

'And it's not just Tom,' Julia continues. 'Where's Gail?'

George knows where she is. Out there, on a pedallo, half naked, with a Greek.

'George?'

He knew this would happen, of course. Gail is curious, uncontrollable, very attractive, he has to admit, but she is also headstrong, stupid and vain. Just like her mother. He storms out of the door and down the stairs to the beach, where he sees Tom, stooping by one of the holes in the side of the house. 'What in the hell are you doing? And where in the hell have you been?'

'Shh!' The boy demands. 'It's a cat and it's dying.' Tom peers inside and suddenly there is a flash of light.

'Damn you, Tom! That's my camera.'

Tom stands up and turns to his father. Eleven years old. Curious, like his sister, eyes wide open. 'Yes, I took it. You know, take some pictures.' George swipes the camera from the boy's hands. 'Don't ever do it again.'

'Jeez, what's got into you?'

George wanders to the water's edge. His son is an aberration, with the morals of a hardened criminal and the accent of an American street kid. He hears the boy come up to him. 'Hi, Dad.' There is silence. 'Mum's pretty mad at you. I heard her.'

'When?'

'Just now.'

'How do you know?'

'She called you a little shit, and then threw your shoes out of the window. That kind of stuff. Don't worry. I picked them up.'

'She's tired,' George says by way of explanation.

They look together across the water. A breeze has come up and the sea is rougher. Swimmers leave the water, and George says, 'The light will go soon.'

'It's a neat place,' Tom says appreciatively. And George looks down on his son, and says, 'Yes, it is. By the way, which shoes did she throw out of the window?'

Martin Rushton arrives in Tiryns tired and in a foul temper. The confused, teeming awfulness of Athens airport in the early hours of the morning, followed by the three hour journey in the coach has done little to allay his fears about this holiday. He had never wanted to come to Greece. It was Maeve who had made the decision, Maeve in yet another of her incomprehensible moods, endlessly silent, restless. 'Mr Rushton? Mr Rushton?' He hears his name called out from the front of the bus where Louise, the courier, stands next to the driver. She beckons him. 'This is where you get out. The end of the journey. Also you, Mrs Simmons, of course. Mrs Simmons and party.' 'Right at the bloody end of the bloody beach,' Martin says under his breath as he sets foot on the street. Louise looks down at a rather small and overweight man, fortyish. His face is slightly blotched and his thinning hair is untidy. She smiles engagingly at him, and says, 'See you this evening. At 'The Welcome'. Don't forget.' He mumbles back at her and makes for The Delphi.

Maeve is not there in person, although she is

there, recognisably, in the room. As at home, as in every single room she ever enters, the place is a mess. Her clothes are half unpacked, knickers under the bed, towels on the bed, straps and legs of trousers spilling out of a half open suitcase. The dressing table is covered with her toiletries, mascara, face cream, lipstick. As he had expected the room itself is bare, basic. He tries to think of other words. Adequate? Acceptable?

'Hullo, Maeve,' he says. He puts his suitcase on one small empty part of the bed and unpacks. His shorts, his T-shirts and ordinary short-sleeved shirts are all neatly ironed and in tidy piles. His hands, thick, fleshy hands covered in short blonde hair, move quickly, placing most of the clothes onto two empty shelves in the old cupboard that stands uncertainly against the white plastered wall. His shoes, highly polished, and bought specially for the holiday, he places at the bottom of the cupboard.

It is ten o'clock in the morning. He goes to the balcony and looks out. He stares critically. As a younger man he has seen other beaches, Calangute in Goa, the empty solitary beaches of undiscovered Samui in the Gulf of Thailand and the vast emptiness of Lion Bay on the island of Phuket before the tourists arrived, and the memory of these places stay with him. They are memories of nature as an ordered force, with the capacity to arrange trees and water, to arrange the land itself in ways which are without question visually totally correct. And these places, visited long ago, remain as refuges, places to retire when alone, places to reorder his thoughts, places that allow him access into their own ordered patterns.

Now, he sees two islands, sitting at the head of the Bay of Argos, one small and with a chapel on its summit, the other about a kilometre in length, rising into two great peaks in the middle. He sees still water, covered in small craft. He sees a great sweep of land going west and south, past the ancient massive rock fortress of Assini, covered in orange groves. And it is all strangely quiet.

At the desk he asks if anyone knows where his wife is. He is directed to the outside bar, where a young waitress, dark and with long black hair, tells him that she had been there in the corner, but that she had left. The girl shrugs her shoulders. 'Maybe she went to look for you.'

The thought that he should get some sleep is at first quite strong, but he is overwhelmed by the thought of having to arrange the bed, and decides against it. He next thinks of having a drink, which is a suggestion he finds much easier to deal with. He pulls a bottle of scotch out of a shoulder bag, then sits on the balcony and pours a large measure into a plastic cup. 'Must get some glasses,' he says to himself. He drinks quickly, and pours himself another. 'That's better. The world would be an awful place without it. Couldn't live with Maeve, for a start. Shouldn't live with her, really.'

He now feels in a much better mood and whistles while he pulls off the clothes he has been travelling in and replaces them with shorts and a clean, light blue cotton shirt. 'Sandals? Where are you? Ah. No socks. Socks and sandals are definitely naff. But it would enrage Maeve. Why not? There we go. Naff little socks. Maeve will be furious. Wonderful.'

Later, he walks up from the hotel onto the narrow road that leads back into town. He sees evidence of a great deal of new building. The land rises steeply on his left, while on the right it slopes over a distance of about fifty metres before it reaches the beach. On the right of the road there are old low buildings, with cracked and faded red tiles on the roofs that come down almost to head level of those walking past. The outside walls are rough and painted white. The windows have green and blue wooden shutters, though most have been unpainted for years. In the doorways, and outside at small tables, are old men and women, the women dressed in black, with black scarves wrapped around their hair and faces. Two old men look up from their coffee, and as they scrutinise him he feels unsettled in a way he has not felt for years. Behind these older houses, along the narrow alleys that climb up the hillside, are individual houses and small blocks of apartments, with green shrubbery growing profusely over the walls and red and blue flowers offsetting the inevitable white, blue and green of the buildings. Higher up still, on barren steep hillside, new apartment blocks are in the process of construction. The land is dry, and rocky. The half built apartment blocks are brown and grey, like the land itself. On the right side of the main road as he walks into town there are gift shops and one or two small cottages, and behind them small private houses lining the alleys that go down to the beach front.

He walks slowly, lifted by the scotch, his body moving almost effortlessly, as though the suppressed tiredness has numbed him. The street begins to get busier. There is a supermarket, then a small hotel, and then a travel agency. The road swings gently, and he finds himself in the main street itself, the original centre of the old fishing village, a stretch no more than four hundred metres long, which now in this busiest time of the year is full of tourists, standing idly, sitting in the open cafes and bars, shopping, fingering sun cream and post cards and beach gear, and leering at wooden and metal satyrs with vast erections, satyrs with pop up organs, satyrs chasing, satyrs possessing.

From time to time he stops and actively searches for his wife, though he imagines she is more likely to be on the beach. Odd, that she wasn't there to welcome him. Slightly disturbed he stops at a bar and orders a drink.

His efforts to remember the day fail. Several times during his life he has forgotten great blocks of time, but these have inevitably been at night - times when he has been out with a friend or with a stranger met casually in a bar, in Callao, or St Michel, or the Reeperbahn, and then miraculously found himself back in his hotel the next morning, in bed, not knowing how he had returned. This is the first time he has forgotten an entire day. When he comes to he is sitting in a rather dark and nearly empty bar. He is at the bar itself, and there is a dead cigarette in his fingers. 'Holy shit,' he says quietly.

'You OK?' the barman enquires. He is a large, broad faced man and he is evidently amused.

Martin nods. 'I think so. Must have fallen asleep.'

'My friend, you fell asleep five or six hours ago.'

'I did?'

'You were with a woman. German, I think. In another bar. You were talking and she was talking, and then you closed your eyes. Bang. Finish. She was very pretty. Nice legs.'

'What happened to her?' He rubs the back of his neck. His watch tells him it is ten o'clock at night. He wonders about Maeve.

'Don't worry. My brother went with her. She was interested in you, I think, but you were asleep, and then my brother came. So, anyway, my friend. I brought you here. How you feel? You want a drink?'

'I think I ought to find my wife. But I'll have a drink first.'

When he gets back to the hotel it is nearly one o'clock in the morning. Maeve is asleep. He stumbles over her suitcase as he reaches for the bed and she wakes up. 'I saw you, you bastard,' she says.

'You were trying to get inside the pants of a German bitch.'

'I don't remember a thing,' he admits quietly.

'How was the flight?' she whispers.

'Bloody awful.'

'Yes, isn't it?'

'Are you having a good time?' he asks.

'Yes.'

'Do you love me?'

'Probably,' she says quietly. It is enough, and he sleeps.

THE DIARY OF JULIA MOORE. HER HOLIDAY, ON THE PELOPONNESE

SATURDAY

I have sworn to be honest in keeping this diary about my holiday, not because I am naturally honest, but because I feel a need to atone for the basic dishonesty that underscores each day of my normal life. It all began, I suppose, when I allowed George to continue his education while I stopped mine, so letting him believe that I wanted nothing more than to stay at home and raise his children. And the dishonesty has continued during all these years of smiling at the evil little creep at Dixon and Brown, accepting it all in exchange for a miserly financial return, but enough so that the damned washing machine can be repaired, or the ancient gas cooker can finally be trailed to the dump and replaced with something that I don't have to try to disguise every time a friend sets foot in the kitchen.

And when George says he doesn't like the way that man watches me, I've always lied, and said that dear old Lawrence Brown is such a sweet old thing, he can't be serious.

Well, I am serious.

This is not a good beginning to this diary. The journey. God, it was awful. We arrived at Gatwick at nine in the evening and left six hours later. Gail disappeared for two hours until Tom found her talking to an Arab. She said she was discussing Palestine, but I know my daughter and she doesn't have a clue about Palestine. Tom said he thought they were holding hands which, if true, I told her, I thought was pathetic. George, who's always a fool in these situations, laughed and Gail said that if he ever let her down in public when we arrived in Tiryns then she was going to leave us. Then George went to the loo and changed into a flaming red Hawaiian shirt, shorts and plastic sandals. That made me mad. He'd promised not to change till we got to Greece, but typically he'd decided to make a fool of himself sooner, rather than later. On the flight George slept. The truth, now that we are dealing with truth, is that I am married to a man who has never grown up, and have two children who show every sign that they have inherited a similar inclination.

We arrived in Athens at six in the morning.

There was a bus, and a three hour journey which the brochure hadn't mentioned. I hated the whole bloody thing and wanted to go back to Silbury. Not that I'll ever admit that to George, of course. And I had forgotten, or probably never knew, that going on holiday means spending time with people you would normally spend a lifetime running away from. A talkative old trout by the name of Betty, with a frail older companion who can only have come here to die, for example. Why do airlines take the risk of letting them on the plane? Must avoid them at all costs. I seem to remember that they're staying at The Delphi. Then a woman who is staying above us at the villa. Two children, like us. But will we like them? I doubt it. There's an affair or two, it seems. A young man with an older woman, and another woman's husband with another man's wife. You can always tell; they always look so bloody happy. I can even remember names; Mr Jones and Mrs Hillier, with a young girl from a previous marriage in tow. The bus was awful and the driver was a maniac, pumping his twin tone horn on the open roads and screaming at huge speeds round village corners, scattering goats, chickens and children.

Greece is a dry sort of place. There's honey advertised on the roadside, so there must be a lot of bees. I've only seen wasps. There is a man called Bullock, who is going to be a terrible bore, not that anyone could be more boring than George.

When we arrived in Tiryns we found it beautiful, white, quiet, blue and green, and I thought with disgust and perhaps sadness of our lives wrapped up at home in that awful Darling Close, and that awful little house. Gail disappeared almost immediately as I knew she would, and wouldn't say where she'd been when she reappeared, but not even Gail could have been up to much after no sleep, and that appalling bus ride.
If Gail ever goes topless I shall scream at her. In public, if I have to. Bloody little Tom disappeared and nicked George's camera. We found out that there's a cat dying under the villa, and of course Tom had to find it. George went to get rid of it, but failed as usual. It's still there, dying or dead, I don't know which, but now it's dark and George is snoring, and the island in front is lit up with floodlights.

It is magical.

I mustn't drink any more ouzo tonight.

TWO

The Moores miss 'The Welcome', which the courier, Louise, arranges for each Saturday intake of guests. How she could have ignored those signs plastered over the walls of the apartment, or forgotten the announcements and reminders on their journey in from the airport. Julia does not know how to explain, except that she had been tired, distraught too because of the children, and George, well George had been hung over, tired, asleep and useless.

On the Sunday morning George visits Louise, who sits behind a not very smart desk in a small office furnished with a fan, a cupboard full of much used paperbacks and an old rattan chair by the door. She is reading and picks at a bowl of grapes. A vast flowing dress falls from two strings over her shoulders, wide freckled shoulders, George notices, below an open face and abundant strawberry blonde hair. 'Hi.' George stands in front of her and announces himself. 'Oh, hi! You missed 'The Welcome' last night. You can't hide anything from me, Mr Moore.'

George is wary. 'Yes. Sorry. Miss anything?'

Louise puts down the book. 'Not much. Usual

warnings. Don't do this and don't do that. Me trying to sell you something. Want to go on the boat trip? There's still room. Tiryns gets full of Greeks on Sundays. Boat leaves at ten. Half an hour's time.'

'What about other days?'

'Just Sundays. It's the Greeks from Athens,' she says. 'They come to escape the heat. They fill the place up.'

Outside, George has noticed that it is already twenty four degrees, and it is only half past nine. 'I don't mind the Greeks. They're fine. Socrates. Agamemnon. All that lot. No, they're fine. Actually, it's about a cat. A dead cat.'

'Oh, shit.' Louise reaches for the phone. 'Black and white?'

'Yes. How did you know?'

'Georgios' cat. The damn thing's been dying for days.' She picks up the phone, dials, and seconds later screams out what George can only assume is a barrage of abuse. She slams down the phone. 'He's basically stupid, that's the problem.'

'Was that him? Georgios? Who is he, anyway?'

'Georgios owns the taverna next to you. And your villa. No, that was Alex.'

'Alex?'

'Yes, Alex. Anyway, how can I help you? Did you read about the trip to Spetses? Or Hydra? Or both?'

'Actually, it's only about the cat. Maybe I didn't explain very well.' George is conscious of a slight heaviness in the front part of his brain. Someone had drunk the best part of a bottle of ouzo the night before. Had it been him? 'The cat,' he repeats. 'The black and white one. My wife is going spare.' He grins, seeking sympathy. What in the hell brings a twenty year old out here, to sit in this office, and wait for people to come in and talk about dead cats?

'I knew it would happen,' she says philosophically. 'Didn't stand a dog's chance. Personally, I'd have drowned it ages ago. There's enough water, for God's sake.'

'Could you, well, do something about it?'

She fixes him with a smile. 'Sure.'

'You're Australian,' he says.

'Actually, no. Auckland. Don't worry, I'll fix it. Where is it? The cat.'

'In a hole. You know, just where the villa and the sand, the beach...'

She nods. 'I know it. Georgios' bitch pupped there last year. Oh, by the way, George. Everything OK? Room clean?' She stands by the desk. 'Coming to Greek Night?'

George comes to the decision that Louise has a

vision of reality which might take some getting to used to but, he thinks, he likes her. Be positive. He smiles. 'It's Louise, isn't it? Look, thanks about the cat. Oh, and something else. I need some drachs. Drachmas. It's Sunday.'

'It is,' Louise says chirpily. 'But that doesn't mean anything.' She opens a drawer. 'How much?'

'You can?'

'Sure.' He changes thirty thousand drachmas and pockets the money. 'Look, Louise. About the cat. The thing is, Mrs Moore, Julia, my wife, gave me rather specific instructions. She'd like to know what's going to happen.'

Louise shuts the drawer. 'I'll get Alex to get rid of it. He'll take it up the dump. Oh, and George? Mr Moore? What about that trip to Hydra? Food on board, wine, as much as you like. Swimming. The lot. Skinny dipping, if you like.'

'You going?' he asks. He grins, and for the first time since those numbing moments after arriving at Gatwick begins to feel good, at ease. Louise twists her mouth. 'Mr Moore, I've got a boy friend.'

'Oh, I see. Is that Alex?'

'Alex? Christ, no. He's a creep.'

Louise sells him tickets to Hydra and Greek Night, and George leaves her and walks into the sunlight, remembering only a dress emblazoned with small white flowers, and eyes which were the palest blue, quite cold, quite bored. Sunday morning is very quiet in Tiryns, but many of the shops in its long, narrow main street are already open. George walks past them - water melons, rubber sandals, postcards of cats, white walls and blue sea, blue sky, green doors. Then down an alleyway, flippers, snorkels, fishing nets, cheap brass Greek soldiers of an unknown century BC, yet more satyrs with amazing organs, Christ where did they get all that blood, and then cats, cats crying out from half open gates, small puddles of water and what might just be urine. Then high above the walls the intense blue of the sky, and out of the shadows stabs of intense heat and light.

He pushes the gate, and goes through the back. Julia is making coffee. 'It's going up the dump,' he says.

She nods. 'Thank God for that.'

Julia lies on the beach. Tom is playing with Nicos from the apartment next door. She is comforted by his conversation, just a metre away at the water's edge.

'Me. Silbury. Very small town in England.'

'England,' Nicos repeats knowledgeably. 'TottnamLivpoolEvton.'

'Where do you live? Gotta sister? I've got one. She's called Gail. What's yours called?' Julia eavesdrops on them. Arrogant little Anglo-Saxon sod.

Gail has disappeared, of course. But Gail, as she is reminded often, and now reminds herself, is fifteen. 'They got married when they were fifteen in the middle ages, mother. Had babies.'

Julia feels uneasy about Gail on this holiday. Shadows pass by; a body sinks close, puffs and sighs. 'George? Oh, I'm sorry. I thought it was my husband.'

'We met yesterday. Jo Bullock.' He nods in the direction of a woman to one side. 'And this is my wife, Mary. Couple of kids. That's Tracy, over there. And there's David. Young chip off the old block.' He pauses, then changes tack. 'Hot?' It is neither a clear question, nor a clear statement. Julia eases up on her elbows. George come and take me away, for God's sake! I don't want to talk to him, or her. Like their mother, the children are silent. They lie next to her, watching her daub herself with white protection, nose, forehead, chin, elbows, shoulders, thighs, calves. Julia watches, in spite of herself, and notices that the woman, Mary, the man's wife, has a pretty face, which after the anointing she hides behind dark glasses.

'David, do the same as your mother,' Jo Bullock

commands. 'And you too, Tracy.' He adjusts a white floppy hat and leans across to Julia. She senses him, feels him far too close, and she hates the smile that comes up so easily, turning his face into a cheerful, grinning, overhealthy advertisement for cleanliness. 'Nice place.' And of course he would have said that, wouldn't he? And she agrees. 'It's beautiful.' Where do they come from, these Bullocks. But it is he who asks her. 'Where do you come from?' She has an awful vision of Darling Close, running its tidy little bricks and lawns round the western edge of Silbury, and it numbs her. But it is Tom who answers. 'Silbury,' he says loudly. 'It's in Wiltshire.' He stands beside Julia protectively, shaking water over her legs. Nicos, his companion, is small, brown, wide eyed. Julia likes his face, and examines the compact, firm little body.

'He's Nicos. He's Greek,' Tom announces, and stands firmly between the Bullock family and his mother.

'Hello, Nicos.'

Nicos grins.

'Where's Gail, Tom?'

'Is that your daughter? the man asks. 'About fifteen, long black hair? She's on a pedallo.'

Julia nods. 'That's her.' She has the feeling that the man's been watching them.

'Silbury, eh? Heard of it, but never been there. Farming?' She wishes she'd brought her sunglasses. Times like this make her see the sense of a veil, a yashmak, privacy from the silly intrusion of unwanted males; this man here, and at home, Lawrence Brown. 'We don't. Farm, I mean. But others do, yes.'

'I'm sorry,' he continues cheerfully, 'but I missed your name. You weren't at 'The Welcome'. She's good, that Louise.'

'Julia. Julia Moore.' She introduces herself awkwardly, and then rushes on, saying, 'My husband is George.' Who joins them, wielding a second beach umbrella.

'This will do the trick,' he announces confidently, digging into the sand with the pole.

'Here. Let me help.' He is joined by Jo Bullock, who reaches for the pole and urges it deeper and deeper into the sand, like a puppydog digging furiously for reward. He grunts, and his body rolls in pleasure at the physical activity. 'Ha!' He is pleased. George and Julia stand back and watch as he finishes off the work, belly moving, large fat thighs rolling, moustache curved in the middle of his smiling, happy face. 'There you go! Up and ready.' His hand shoots out and clasps George's limp unready fingers. 'Jo Bullock.' George nods, and withdraws a little. 'George,' he murmurs his own name. 'Good to meet you, George. That's my family. There.' George follows the direction of the outstretched arm and sees three silent shapes, reading behind sunglasses.

'George?' Julia whispers. 'How much?'

'What?'

'This thing. The umbrella. We've already got one. The red one.' They sit next to each other and her voice is urgent. 'Oh, I don't know. I got some other things. Credit card.'

'What things?'

'Flippers. Snorkel. Things like that.'

'George, be careful with the money. You promised.'

'And this thing,' he says, ignoring her. He leans across and shows her a small bronze Attican taking a woman from behind. 'Like this, see.' He works the man back and forward. 'I thought I might give it to Jane. Or you could give it to that Brown man. Or I could give it to Margaret Tanner, at the school. She'd like it.'

Julia works her teeth. 'It's a bit silly, isn't it? How do you know she'd like it?' 'Not silly at all,' he says, replying only to her first comment. 'Anyway, they've always liked it this way out here. For centuries. Natural pastime. No problem about bad breath, that sort of thing.'

'Oh, shut up, George. You're meant to be a

headmaster. Anyway, you shouldn't stereotype so much.'

'Being historically accurate doesn't deserve that kind of dismissal,' he protests. 'Let's see what he thinks.' He turns to Jo Bullock and calls out his name.

'George, don't!' Julia whispers furiously. 'Don't show me up!'

George demonstrates the plaything to Jo, who is confused, and coughs, and eyes his family. George shrugs his shoulders and withdraws. The offending article is dropped into a beachbag. 'I'll give it to your mother,' he says finally. Julia ignores the comment, and is secretly thankful. Perhaps now that Bullock man will disappear in search of other playfellows. 'What about the cat?' she asks quietly.

'I told you. Chap called Alex will take it to the dump.'

'When?'

'Don't know.' George looks at his watch. 'Time for a beer.'

She restrains him with one hand. 'Where's Gail?'

'On a pedallo.'

'Alone?'

He stands up and scans the sea. He can imagine that when the wind gets up things could be difficult. An image of wind and wave and water pouring into his body catches him unawares and he tenses, enough to catch his wife's attention and bring puzzlement to her face. She sees the headmaster of St Mary's, strangely at this moment with some authority standing there and staring out to sea. St Mary's Primary School, once a very Christian institution, now run by a bunch of meatheads and middle class do-gooders. Well, it's a living. For him. As for herself, there is resentment. She should retrain, but they can't afford it, and so she's left with the computer, and the filing, and the routine, and the dank smell of cloying, ageing maleness.

'Where are you going, George?' She tries to dampen the unexpected panic in her voice.

'Beer.'

'What about me?'

'Come along.'

She runs to join him. Tom is safe with Nicos. The Bullock man raises a limp left hand in their direction. Gail is on a pedallo. There, a hundred metres or so away in front of the Hotel Delphi stand two elderly women. In the middle ground between them the woman with the young man takes off her top. Breasts so firm, at her age. The young man laughs. They're in love. And then a vaguely familiar voice from another young man, boy, calls out behind her. 'I used the factor six, then put it in the cupboard.' 'It wasn't there,' a younger voice counters. 'That's because you used it this morning but didn't put it back.' 'No, I didn't use it.' 'Yes, you did.' The younger brother carries a fishing net. The older one has a snorkel sticking out of the top of his head, attached by the strap on his mask.

Julia reaches for George's hand as the two pass. 'Is there a father?' she asks.

'I haven't seen one. Yet,' he adds.

She clasps his hand. 'Sorry I've been snappy.'

'You haven't. Let's get that beer.'

'I didn't tell you. I bought tickets for Greek Night.'

'Oh, when?'

'Tonight.'

'Greek Night?' Julia has visions of shattered plates, of George misbehaving, of endless drink. 'Do we have to?'

They are sitting in the corner of the patio of The Ship, which strategically holds down one of the main centres of the beach front. It is a modern concrete structure painted green and white, with wooden benches, tables and chairs set to one side of a large wooden bar inside the large fan-cooled interior. But it is more popular for the tables and chairs that cluster under umbrellas on the large patio facing the beach. It is now eleven o'clock. The beach is crowded; Louise's promise has been fulfilled. Tiryns is besieged by Athenians, escaping the intolerable concrete city. They sprawl along kilometres of beach, tucked into the few natural shadows provided by beached fishing vessels, and the steel and concrete skeletons of half-finished buildings. The sand itself is covered by bright umbrellas, concentrated in even greater numbers outside favourite tavernas. The Anchor. Vangelis'. Tom's. Nestor's. The Bridge. The Blue Moon. And incongruously in the middle of it all a long low taverna run by an exiled Londoner, called 123, Mile End Road. Confused tourists lie among them, burning slowly, the ones who have chosen to stay, who have ignored the invitations to swim, drink and be happy elsewhere, on another beach, on one of the islands, anywhere.

'Families,' George says enigmatically. He has his feet up, a book on his lap, a large beer beside him. He raises his glass to his wife. 'Ours?' she questions. 'No. Here. These families. Grandmothers, great grandmothers, kids, the lot. Nice.' 'You're sentimental,' she retorts. 'It's the beer talking. What about our family?' He picks up his book. 'George? Talk to me. What about our family?' 'OK, ours too,' he allows. 'But it's different here. Greek families are different.' 'You mean you wouldn't want my grandmother with you on holiday?' she persists. 'No, of course not,' he replies. 'She's dead.' 'That's not what I meant, George. What's the book?'

He shows her, and then exclaims, 'My God, look at that lot!' He reacts to the shrieking at the water's edge.

George gets to his feet and she joins him quickly. A huge plastic hippopotamus with the name of a bank in Salzburg written across its side rocks up and down four or five metres out to sea, its legs pointing helplessly upwards. A bald and badly burned pursuer thrashes in the water just a little way behind it. 'Mad,' George announces solemnly. Julia sniggers. The man and his prey are not alone. The plastic beast is accompanied by others like it, in its own form, and other creatures, mammoths and crocodiles among them. Around them, temporarily astride or, if in the water, screaming at each other and desperately trying to mount, is a large group of men and women, their eyes hidden behind goggles, their skin blotched red, the intensity of their labours blinding them to the attention they are beginning to gain from the beach.

'He won't make it,' George pronounces,

absorbed by the pursuit. Julia laughs aloud, full and heavy laughter that is echoed elsewhere on the patio.

Dimitris, the owner of The Ship, stands beside them. He is a short, tidy man. He shakes his head. 'Crazy people. Crazy.'

'You know them?' George asks.

'Sure. They come every year. The same men, the same women. Sometimes a new wife, a new husband, new kids. But the animals are always different. Giraffe, elephant, big fish, how do you say?' He draws a figure in the air. 'Whale?' George suggests. 'Yes, whale. Any bloody animal. Always the same. Crazy.' Dimitris touches his head.

The pursuit continues, the hippo ever more elusive, the pursuer undaunted. 'That guy is special,' Dimitris confides. 'Bank manager. Off his head.' George agrees silently, and watches in amazement as a yelling bundle of red flesh lands atop the hippo with a scream of joy. The water around the beast and its rider froth, as hands go up to meet him and shrieks of jubilation and congratulation engulf the beach. Inevitably victory is short lived. Slowly and without much grace the hippo slides beneath the water, throwing its rider into the arms of a hysterical delighted female attendant. The event is greeted with a huge burst of applause from almost a hundred metres of beach, which so astounds the Austrian bankers that the entire group falls silent, and turns in bewilderment towards its unexpected audience.

'I want one,' Julia says helplessly.

'What? A hippo?'

'Any of them.'

The Austrians disperse, leading their impossible mounts to another, more distant part of the beach.

Julia thinks of the evening to come. 'Promise me something, George? Please don't get drunk tonight.' George considers the request and says, 'What makes you say that?' 'I just don't want you to, that's all. Promise?'

He looks out across the water. 'Can you imagine this place with triremes in the bay?' he asks.

'Why not? Look at that.'

A huge cabin cruiser has anchored two hundred metres out. About it on either side there are scores of other craft. And on the horizon, but approaching at speed, the hydrofoil from Athens comes into view, standing up on its legs like a giant spider.

In the February of 1984 Martin Rushton had been sitting one afternoon on the terrace of the

Nuangruan restaurant in Pattaya, watching a large junk drop anchor just a mile to the north of Go Larn, the big island that lies just off the Thai coast in front of the sprawl and desecration of Pattaya Beach. In that year he had been an eager, taut, energetic person, still much of a schoolboy at the age of thirty; blonde, blue eyed, and very confident. Sitting at a table near the railings that surrounded the terrace he appeared a slight figure, his rather spare body slightly slouched. He was smoking. A copy of Reynold's 'Woman of Bangkok' lay unopened in front of him. At a table just a few metres away there was a single woman, tall, dark haired, wearing white shorts. Large, round sunglasses were propped on the top of her head. She was totally absorbed in writing, which she did, he observed, at enormous speed.

She wrote in an exercise book. The wind blew. The pages rose and flapped, and her pen fell onto the wooden planks of the floor. As she looked down to find it, so did he, and they smiled at each other. Later, Maeve Philips asked him where he was from in England, and he had told her that he preferred to think of himself as a European. Her eyes had focused on him, lit, sparkled, and her mouth had whispered 'Bullshit.' Now, ten years later, Martin Rushton sits on their balcony at The Delphi Hotel, and remembers the day they'd met.

'Do you remember the first word you said to me?' he calls out to her.

She is sitting in the room on the bed, reading through some notes. She lifts her head and looks out to the balcony. She remembers the day well, the precise moment of meeting him, the words, the meals that followed. The routine, that with him, had somehow not been a routine at all. She had laughed at him, secretly. A European? He was, so precisely, English. But in those early days she had probably been in love with him. Why not? His energy had infatuated her. She had loved his attention, she had drowned herself in his images of Paris, Amsterdam and Madrid, and she had been fascinated by his ability to switch backwards and forwards in French, and German and Italian.

And Martin had money.

'What did I say? I've forgotten,' she says quietly, patiently.

He comes in from the balcony and sits on the bed next to her

'You said, 'Bullshit'.'

She nods. 'It sounds about right.'

'Already?' he says, indicating the exercise book.

'Yes. Already.'

Maeve was successful when he had met her. Now, her travel articles and short pieces on the vagaries of the British abroad are to be found in magazines throughout the English speaking world. Their friends see them as solid examples of the essence of the eighties. Monied, hard working, successful.'

'Anyone in particular?' he enquires further.

'Yes. There's a primary school headmaster and his wife. The Moores. They came in on the same plane as you. I spotted them yesterday.'

'Maeve?' He leans towards her. His face is flushed, and she knows he's been drinking. 'Maeve, why did you say you'd forgotten what you'd said to me that day in Pattaya when I know damn well you knew what you'd said.'

'Because I wanted to piss you off. Oh, get off the bed, Martin.' Martin wanders back out to the balcony. There had been an awful day a month ago, walking down the Quai Voltaire in Paris, when he'd been overcome by a distressing, sickly fear. It had only been later, over a large brandy in a cafe in St Michel that he had become suspicious about the cause. It was the French. They were beginning to alienate him. Now, he stares out at Aphrodite, and his eyes climb her giant breasts. His memory is full of islands, and they float around his dreams like sirens: Samui, Penang, Socotra, Gomora, Zanzibar. Islands peopled by Maeve. English men and women in funny hats and shorts. Gin and lager and lemonade. Those funny accents of the white Barbadians. Those yuppie hippies in Sri Lanka. Maeve has watched them all, and from time to time has written him in, referring to him smirkingly in short asides.

'This is Martin, my husband. He's a European.'

And then there are the men, chased and harried, year after year. Her men. He has memories of Maeve, like a sleek black cat, stalking them along Asian alleyways and through white bright South American squares, hunting them in Delhi, taunting them in St Telmo, as if sex in Buenos Aires had been invented by her alone, and then, at the end, when she has them at her feet, playing with them, until she becomes bored and tosses them aside.

'You know that nothing happens,' she had assured him. 'I don't do anything.' And in a way he is used to it, the endless flirtation and openness, the enthusiastic and often confused response, the final and always predictable rupturing of an apparently close relationship. 'It's how I work,' she'd told him, 'I can't help it. I'm not an artist but I am a journalist, and I have my ways of working. This is me. It's how I do it.'

There is a young woman on the beach, about eighteen years old. Her hair is blonde and thick. He watches her strip off her top and stride out to the water. Her movements catch him unawares, so that he does not see Maeve slip out of the room and stand beside him. She nuzzles close. 'I see you,' she whispers. 'Can we make love?' he replies. 'No.' He continues to watch the girl. What, he wonders would an average Italian male in his position do with a wife who had become totally disinclined to any form of sexual encounter?

He ought to talk to her about it. But he won't.

'Yesterday,' he says. 'Why didn't you meet me when I arrived?'

The Bullocks' older child sits totally still, with the pillow propped up behind her. She is good at these silences; they are long practised. She watches her mother prepare for Greek Night, watches the hair dryer move carefully across the hair, watches the familiar movements in front of the mirror - the head bent one way, then the other, the silent, still confrontation between her mother and the untidy, half clothed reflection in the mirror.

The child stares at the reflection through half shut eyes. On the bed next to her, her brother is equally motionless. Less hopeful than his sister he has already changed into his blue and white striped pyjamas. There will be no Greek Night for them. It will be consigned, like so much else, to events they hear about, but which officially never exist.

Later, much later, their father will come back, and he'll be drunk. And he'll sit down on one of their beds and talk. But again, these conversations do not officially take place. They drift about in the dark, phantoms that vanish with the daylight. He'd told them once of going to Cairo, and being introduced to a famous Arab, and the children had suddenly seen their father as a man of substance, astride a camel, conquering the desert. In the dark the boy had stared at the lone still figure of his father, dressed in white, pulling hard at the camel's head, then heard the quiet, inevitable whisper, saying, 'Don't tell her that I woke you. Mum's the word, eh?'

And so they say nothing, and he never reminds them, and in the end these dismembered ramblings remain apocryphal. The children stay awake at night, and have done for years each time the parents go out, waiting for the father to return, and then counting, to hundreds and thousands, till the mother pushes open the door. They never know where she has been, and they never ask. The girl remembers when they had left Gatwick. It had been, unusually, a perfectly wonderful day. Her mother had let her help with the packing, finally placing clothes that had been bought carefully week after week during the summer into the new suitcases her father had brought back in the car one Saturday afternoon. Her brother had pretended to be reading, but was really watching mother and sister. The silence had been warm, inviting, and she had found herself staying close to her mother, following her round the house, stopping off to help with the meals when her mother muttered about food, running to the door when the bell rang and the postman had come with a letter.

But her mother had pushed past her and said, 'I'll take that. It's for me. It's mine.' And then disappeared for nearly ten minutes. The potatoes had boiled over, and the girl had worked hard at the stain on the stove before it was noticed. When her mother returned she was flushed.

'The potatoes boiled over,' the girl said, and her mother nodded, and suddenly reached out for the child, putting one arm round her and pulling her tight. It was only then that the girl's curiosity had been really roused, as she wondered what that letter had said and who had said it. Wanting to share what had happened she had told her brother later, upstairs. 'It was from a man,' she had said.

'Of course it wasn't.' The boy had inspected the suitcases and stared at the family name printed large on the luggage tags. BULLOCK. 'I hate being a Bullock,' he had added under his breath.

That evening at Gatwick the Bullocks had sat in

a small group in the departure lounge, waiting patiently. As her mother dresses, the girl remembers those last moments at Gatwick. There had been three young men wandering round the vast lounge of the terminal waving glasses of beer, and she remembers her mother saying, 'I hope to God they're not coming with us.' Her mother was wearing a blue flowered dress and a white straw hat. She was a slight figure beside her father, who stood nearby and surprisingly appeared totally lost. Then out of the men's toilets another man had appeared, a large, big nosed man with thinning hair and a visible paunch. The girl saw her mother's eyes grow large. The man was dressed in brown shorts and a large Hawaiian shirt, and the Bullock family watched him march up to a woman sitting alone with a gin and tonic at the bar, and heard her say, 'Damn you, George Moore, how could you!' The distress was broadcast loudly.

Now, on the bed, the girl remembers that man in his Hawaiian shirt, and as if it was he who had given her the strength she says, 'Mum, can we go, just this once?'

There is no answer. The boy lies on the bed, watching a mosquito on the ceiling. The single sheet is a shroud over his slight body. Both children hear the door click. It opens again and a man's voice says, 'Won't be long.'

Julia Moore is dressed in a white trouser top combination, which she had spent best part of an hour lingering over in Bath, on that last trip down there just before the journey out to Greece. George sits next to her. He is proud of his wife; Julia has taken time, and she looks good. The other women haven't failed to notice, either. Good old Julia. Always can be relied on. But can he? He contemplates the immediate future, namely the hours between now, which he estimates to be about nine o'clock, and whatever. He's not sure. He'd had a couple at The Ship during his quick walk when Julia had been in the shower. A couple of ouzos on his own on the balcony when Julia had been putting on her face. Then there was the beer he'd had with Jo Bullock. Odd man, he thinks. There have to be other men to team up with on the beach than Bullock.

The table is laid for thirty, and the Moores nod at those they know. The two Bullocks. Mrs Simmons and her companion. Mrs Preston in the flat directly above them, and her two children. The older woman and the younger man, the lovers. Young Tom who had insisted he be included, dressed up in a black loose shirt and white trousers, silent, observant, and Gail, who had come in late with a young man she had introduced as Stavros.

'Very forward of you,' Bullock had said, nodding at their daughter and her Greek companion. George isn't so sure, and Julia isn't sure at all. But neither replies.

'A friend?' was Julia's rather obvious question to her daughter a little earlier.

'Yes.'

'Greek?'

'Yes. They're mostly Greeks here, Mum.'

'Well. I just hope he behaves,' George heard himself say.

'Dad, it's Greek Night. He's a Greek.'

'So?'

'So he knows how to behave.'

'Good,' George had ended lamely, weighing her logic and finding it faultless. 'Don't get assholed, Dad,' Tom had said, terminating the conversation.

There are others. A couple in their late thirties or early forties, quiet, rather aloof at this stage, she with a red flower in very black hair, long legs, long angular face, and her partner shorter with a rounded face set close to his shoulders. He sits back in his chair and seems restless. His white shirt is open. He wears a gold watch. 'Car salesman,' George whispers to his wife. 'Insurance,' she whispers back. 'BMWs.' 'No, life insurance. She owns a dress shop.' 'Masseuse,' he counters. 'No, too thin.' 'Good legs.' Julia

hesitates then answers, 'You can't see her legs.'
'I've seen them.'
Then there's tall, heavily built Mr Jones and his lady, Mrs Hillier, sun tanned already. The young girl must be hers, George is sure, and says to Julia, 'They've already been to the Bahamas. This is a top up. He's in finance. Money.'

'No, it's a sunbed. She uses it all year round. He's a PE teacher.'

'Don't be daft. He buys and sells.'

'What?'

'Commodities. Orange juice. Fish. Cotton.'

She acquiesces, then says, 'Promise not to get drunk?' He swills a mouthful of retsina. 'Christ, do we have to drink this?' he asks aloud.

The table is set out on the open verandah of The Delphi. The temperature is still in the high twenties but there is a light breeze off the water. The verandah of The Delphi is covered in grapes and gourds, a haven for wasps and other flying things during the day, but now set with small lights angled upwards to pick out those huge bunches of black grapes that fall in apparently limitless abundance from out of the greenery. The water is only a few metres away, separated from them by a narrow concrete path and a slight strip of sand. Immediately to the right and behind them the shadow of the small quiet harbour darkens the water. A few hundred metres away there is another more massive shadow, thrown across the water by the almost full moon moving across the breasts of Aphrodite. Down the bay the smaller island of Coronisi is lit up by floodlights, which pick out the tiny chapel on its wooded summit in a play of blue, and green and orange. The table itself generates noise. There is a buzz of noise between people, even among the Bullocks, Julia notices.

'They're talking,' she whispers to her husband about the Bullocks.

'You can't produce two children without saying anything.'

'I mean they're talking now.'

Mary Bullock is turned towards her husband; his head is inclined towards hers.

'Their children aren't here,' Julia observes.

George reaches for his glass, which is no sooner emptied than filled by a hovering attendant waitress. Two men rush in, hands high above their heads, trays of salad balanced perfectly. 'Greek salad,' they announce loudly. 'Tomatoes, cheese, very good. Yes, very good cheese. Greek cheese, madam? No, not cheddar. Greek cheese. Feta. Olives. Makes your skin healthy, madam. Beautiful.' Eyes sparkle. The trays are piloted expertly onto the table.

'I thought only the Italians did that,' Julia muses aloud. The idle remark drifts clearly through a sudden silence across the table, and is greeted by a slight smile from the Preston woman, and an unexpectedly loud laugh from the partner of the car salesman.

After the laughter she comments huskily, 'They all do it. It's meant to act as an aphrodisiac, lots of banter, that kind of thing. Talk about food is really nothing less than intimate reference to your body, when you think about it. You'll notice it's never directed at the men.'

Julia nods. Not a masseuse. 'Nice tomatoes,' she says to the car salesman, who looks away, and coughs, and Julia doesn't blame him. How in the hell can you continue a conversation that begins like that? She kicks George, smiles at his surprised reaction, asks for help. And he does try. 'Julia loves tomatoes,' he expands affably. 'Big beefy ones, large red ones. Mmm.' He reaches for the retsina. 'You're a shit,' she hisses.

'Don't touch that stuff,' the car salesman warns, indicating the retsina. George's hand drops. The exchange is carried out at an angle across the table, with no concern for the very quiet young couple to the Moores' right, and the retired couple introduced as Terry and Dina Peters on the car salesman's right. Martin Rushton produces a bottle of scotch from beneath his chair and pours into George's glass. The bottle is then proffered to Julia, who declines.

'It kills you, that stuff,' Terry comments on the retsina in a high voice. Incredibly, Julia sees that he is wearing a cardigan, green, heavy knit. His hands rest on the tablecloth, fingers thick, worn, solid. His gaze is firm. Dina Peters is a short woman, who sits absolutely straightbacked, like a wooden doll. She drowns her retsina in defiance.

'Rubbish,' she retorts. 'Greeks drink it.'

'Of course they drink it,' her partner replies reasonably. 'Got to, haven' they? They make the bloody stuff.'

'Have a glass of scotch, Terry,' Martin Rushton says affably.

'Scotch? Thanks. Very decent of you.'

Martin is not a car salesman, Julia decides. Not insurance, either. Then what?

'You be careful with that scotch, Terry,' Dina snaps, eying her husband's glass. Then to the group at large she expands, by saying, 'Scotch isn't good for him. He gets unreasonable.'

The husband snorts. 'Me?' The bottle of scotch is placed on the table, and the now professionless provider produces yet another bottle.

'Can't stand that stuff,' Martin repeats,

indicating the retsina. 'What about that other wine, Demestica?' Julia says. 'Lavatory cleaner,' Terry pronounces. 'Metaxa?' she asks. 'Metaxa?' the old man says loudly. I drank a bottle of that stuff when she,' he points at his wife, 'went off with Larry in Corfu. Worst drink in the world for the head, but it goes down like syrup. Just like syrup. Anyway, I was gutted when she went off, just like that. Bastard, he was.'

George leans across the table towards the small upright woman. A large diamond ring rises fiercely from her left hand. 'You went off with another man?' he asks incredulously. She nods. 'I did, and I'd do it again. That Richard Gere would do, I'd go with him.'

'In Corfu?' George continues.

'That's right.'

'When was that?' George won't give up, and Julia interrupts, saying, 'You've got to excuse my husband. He gets carried away. George!'

'Oh, I don't mind,' Dina Peters says eagerly. 'Last year it was.'

'Two years ago,' her husband corrects her. 'Left me on the first Friday night, with this bloke from Brentwood.' 'Well,' she retorts, dipping a huge piece of bread into the oily remains of her salad, 'so I did. And a right little shit he turned out to be, too.' Julia moves the scotch away from her husband, who reclaims it, pours another and says to Martin Rushton, 'Julia and I, my wife, that is, thought you were a car salesman.' He grins.

Julia erupts. 'Oh, for Christ's sake, George, haven't you got any manners?'

Maeve laughs, and George is delighted. He likes this couple, and he likes her, this black haired, large eyed woman. The smoothness of the skin on her face. He conjures other parts of her, and frolics alone, and in silence.

The night lies heavily on the sea; a boat goes out, the engine is loud, rhythmical. 'Octopus,' Maeve says, indicating the boat, and George hears the word, and repeats it in his head; it is heavy and full and writhes with intimations of other things.

'OK, everybody, now we eat.' A master of ceremonies enters. Alexos, manager of The Delphi, stands in the doorway, small, thick head of hair, trousers and shirt pressed just so. Small, precise moustache. 'Lamb and fish,' the moustache announces.

Then waiters.

'You want lamb or fish?

'Lamb.

'Fish.'

'Excuse me, is this lamb or fish?'

'Fish.'

'Never seen a fish like this before. Look at the

oil.'

'James, I can't eat this.' The young woman of the young couple is pale, and sickening by the second. Julia watches them, early twenties, not a word so far. Just married? She suddenly wants to put her arm out, around both of them. And her husband, James, does not know what to say. There is silence while the group contemplates the dilemma. 'I'm sure it's fine,' he says finally.

'Put it on the ground when they're not looking,' Terry advises. 'The dogs'll eat it.'

'Have a tomato, dear,' Dina says, proffering a large beef tomato on the end of her fork.

'Actually, I don't think she feels very well,' James says apologetically. George knows the problem. Retsina. He eyes the fish on his plate. Through its dead eye, it eyes him back. 'I mean, they eat the stuff,' he hears Terry explain, 'because they get used to it, over the years. Mind you, in Corfu it wasn't any better. Worse than Southend.' The young wife stands up and slips away into the shadows. James is about to follow, but George restrains him. 'She'll be back,' he advises. 'Harvey Wallbangers,' James says, sighing. 'I told her, but she insisted.' His face livens quickly. 'Probably the Viva Maria, now I think about it.'

'Viva Maria?' George puzzles.

James looks at him and explains. 'One measure

tequila, half measure lime juice, quarter measure maraschino, half teaspoon grenadine, half egg white. She had four.' The table is silent, impressed. 'Ah well, there you go, James.' George says. 'Say no more. Don't trust anything south or west of Calais, or any other bloody direction. What do you do at home?'

'Sell houses. Or used to, rather.'

Totally unfairly, George reflects, Julia says, 'George, please don't have anything more to drink. Please. And eat your lamb.'

George stares at his fish, then smiles amiably at the couple across the table, now jobless, nameless; and he catches Julia watching. There is a stain on her shoulder. Oil from the lamb or fish, too high for her to see, best to say nothing. In the morning, maybe, now would be catastrophic. 'Didn't catch your name,' he says to Martin Rushton.

'Oh, Rushton. Martin Rushton.'

And the name is somehow familiar, and so too now is the face, and hers as well. TV? An ad? Margerine? Household soap? 'Baked Beans?' The question escapes, and hangs rootless amidst the conversation, and that flusters him. Shit. He covers quickly. 'Hi, I'm George Moore, I look after boys and girls, not very PC these days, but there you go. Not very good at it, probably, as Julia, there, that one, my wife, will tell you. Headmaster, can't go any higher, actually. Have to wait till death, that sort of thing.'

'Shut up, George.'

'Are you and he, well...' he looks fondly at the woman, and her eyes smile back.

Julia is mortified. 'George, it's none of your business.'

'Oh? Married, you mean? Yes, in fact,' Martin Rushton says, staring hard at Maeve. All of this, this night, this bloody holiday, she'll claim as expenses from the taxman. Research. This poor bloody couple from England. And he quite likes this George, and his wife. The table quietens, till shaken by the sudden summons of a bouzouki.

'Oh Christ,' Terry says, raising his head from apparent torpor, 'I can't stand this bloody dancing.' And Gail gets up and dances with Stavros, and two of the waiters join in.

'We should meet him,' Julia says to her husband.

'Is that your daughter?' Maeve asks her. Such a deep voice, George registers. George is enthralled by the couple. He smiles at Martin. Wonderful man to bring the whisky and save him from drowning in this foul ocean of retsina, and then to bring along such a woman. He smiles with love across the table; his emotion wells out of him, a thick cloud of longing. And then he catches sight of Gail. 'Lovely girl,' he says to no one in

particular, 'but uncontrollable. Won't listen.'
'Do you two talk?' Maeve asks. 'You and your wife?'

There is no doubt about the question, and its directness cuts in a swift and inescapable thrust. Julia watches her husband, listens, is attentive, and waits. And is not surprised when he turns to her and says, 'Ah, do we talk, darling? You? Me? The kids? Christ, we talk all the bloody time. The house is full of talk. Where others have flying ducks and Eiffel Towers and pictures of Aunt Rose in the garden of Hampton Court, Number 6, Darling Close, is full of words.'

'George is now drunk,' Julia announces.

'Is he really a headmaster?' Maeve asks Julia.

'Oh, yes.'

Maeve lights a cigarette and leans across the table. 'Who's that man with the woman in the sunglasses. Does she know it's night?' 'Bullock,' Julia tells her. Her attention wanders and she says aloud, 'Where's Tom?' Tom is asleep, slumped down in his chair, and only the black tuft of his hair is visible above the table top. 'George, you gave him something to drink, damn you.' George nods. 'Of course. If I hadn't he would have taken it, and if he'd taken it he would have taken too much.' 'He's had too much,' she points out. And so has Jo Bullock, who suddenly jumps up, grabs for the back of his chair, misses, sprawls, regains balance, and climbs on the seat. The music hesitates, then continues. Gail and Stavros dance, he leading, she following carefully, oblivious to all onlookers. 'George, shall we go?' Julia says anxiously, waiting for the worst to happen. 'No.' Jo Bullock is red, fullblown, his face thrust forward like a giant turtlehead, quivering. His voice finally bursts out, drowning the music. 'Plates! I want to break plates. Let's have some fun, eh? Maestro, bring on the plates.' His wife rises slowly, pushes her chair back, and leaves.

George watches, his wife, the Bullocks, the couple they have just met, Dina Peters with her glasses held a little in front of her face, eyeing the man on the chair, Mrs Preston, smiling just a little, her two children no longer present, and Mr Jones alert, large and somehow unprepared, sitting close to Mrs Hillier.

'Let's have some fun!'

Julia reaches for George's hand. Alexos, the hotel manager, he who had invited them all to enjoy, hovers uncertainly, and it is in this very unexpected silence that the night is broken by a sudden chanting down the beach. 'Come on you Spuuuurs!

Come on you Spuuuurs!'

'Excuse me, mister.' George looks up and sees Alexos beckoning him. 'Please tell your friend...,' and George protests immediately, 'He is not my friend.' 'Maybe, but he is English.' George admits it, and nods. 'If he breaks just one plate, well, my brother is police captain.' George grins. 'Good job,' he acknowledges. 'Very useful.'

'What did he want?' Julia asks. She is nervous. The music starts again, but not before the chant is repeated, followed by a torrent of abuse.

'Oh, good heavens,' says Dina. 'These Greeks swear just as badly as some of our English boys.'

'They're not Greeks, you daft old trout,' her husband tells her. 'They are English. I'd bloody shoot them, I would.'

Jo Bullock is perplexed. Still standing on the chair he says, 'Well? Let's do something.' His face is blotched red. George goes up to him and reaches out a hand. 'Jo?' The man looks down and grins in recognition. 'We've got a crisis,' George says quietly. 'Crisis? What do you mean, crisis?' 'Those louts,' George says, waving his hand down the beach. 'Oh, shit. Where are they?' Jo stumbles down from the chair. 'You came to the right man, my friend.' Jo Bullock throws his arm round George's shoulders, and pulls him away from the table.

SUNDAY

Today has been merciful. I count myself lucky I did not fight with my children. They are both, as far as I know, asleep here in the same villa as us. George drank too much tonight, but did not disgrace himself. In fact, he was a hero. That awful man Bullock could have created hell but we were saved by the sudden arrival of those three young men. And then dear George, stumbling off with that man onto the beach.

One o'clock in the morning. Stone cold sober. The moon is so bright, those islands are so very close, the water is quite still. Tiryns is far from asleep. Somewhere up the beach I can hear a disco. Cavos or Sweet Youth, if I remember the names correctly. Below me there are earnest voices, two young women, a couple of boys. I think I saw them earlier today, very athletic, and fresh in a way we weren't at that age. I can't imagine what it is like now to be seventeen or eighteen, as relaxed as they apparently are. I felt close to George today as I haven't done for a long time. It is hard suddenly to have to wonder if the man you have dismissed for so long is not so easily to be dismissed. The problem is that I'm not very good at these thoughts, unpractised. These last few years have centred so much around the children. And it is strange to be so far away from that creep back in the office. The Preston woman in the flat above us fascinates me. She is very pretty but somehow quite distant. Not like her children, so vocal. George and I tend to restrain Tom and Gail. Those confrontations with Gail, even Tom's eccentricity, upset me. But that woman up there is calm. I wonder about her husband. Why am I so interested in her that he, whoever he is, has become a question? Because it's unusual for a woman to travel alone with children? No, it's not unusual. He's probably on business. Paris, or New York.

So, tonight was Greek Night. How absurd a name. I had secretly dreaded it but in fact I felt better all evening than for a long time. Gail was there with her man. He seems a very collected young man, polite, and very handsome. He is, I suspect, in his early twenties, and he speaks quite good English. I asked him about that, about where he'd learnt to speak so well, and he had smiled back, very engagingly, 'Oh, here, on the beach.' I shall have to watch her, both of them in fact. Gail is still so young.

Those others, Martin and Maeve. I've seen her before somewhere. Why is it some people are so perfectly sure of themselves there isn't a hint of doubt in what they do? They seem so out of place here, as though they're slumming. Of course, George was fascinated with her, that was obvious, not that he would ever try anything. He hasn't got the guts. But I do like them. Is it because of all these people we are the most similar? Then again, I don't know about that. I bet he doesn't have to run a ten year old Rover. A BMW, more likely. Nor do they live in a place like 6, Darling Close, with that hideous brick front and the tiny lawn that gives George angina every time he gets near the bloody lawn mower.

This place is more beautiful than I could have imagined. For thousands of years those islands out there and the great hill behind have been the same. There has been a Tiryns for centuries. First the Greeks and the Turks, and now the Germans, Austrians, Swedes and us, the British.

I can hear George asleep, turning. We have bought a fan, the last in Tiryns, and it turns noisily. It is another new sound for me, the constant rhythmical moving of air. And there are other new sounds. The cicadas. Music, that at times is so strangely Arab. And water, moving slowly up and slowly down the slight incline of the beach.

When I left the verandah of The Delphi tonight it was to find Tom. Without our noticing he had slipped away, but then so had half the group. Telling Gail I was off in search of her brother I left, first shaking hands with her young man. He said it had been a pleasure meeting me, and he held my hand firmly.

I found Tom down the beach, bent over, then crawling.

'What on earth are you up to?' I demanded.
'Shh!'
'Well?'
'Stalking' he whispered enigmatically.
'No. Bedtime,' I told him.
'No!'
'Yes.'

He grabbed my hand and indicated I should be quiet. Following his other, outstretched, hand I made out a couple in the water, not many metres away. 'They're stark naked,' he said excitedly. I could see it was the older woman and her young lover, standing totally entwined, oblivious to the small voyeur back on the beach. I pulled Tom back. 'Oh, Mum!'

'That's private,' I told him.
'Not if they're doing it in public it isn't.'

Tom complained that I hit him round the ear. I don't remember that detail. And so I came home with Tom, and found George asleep.

There is something too perfect about all this.

THREE

On the Tuesday the Moores go on a boat trip to Spetses and Hydra. They get up early in the morning, George quiet and hung over, clumsily dressing and preparing coffee and toast with measured grunts of good humour. Gail surprises her mother by her willingness, and the energy with which she finds the towels, flippers and snorkels, and packs a thermos of tea and packets of biscuits into a large red plastic cooler.

'You can buy that stuff on board,' Tom says to her in the kitchen.

'Clear off.' She kicks out at him. 'Why aren't you ready?'

'I am ready.'

'No, you're not.'

'Oh, shut up, the pair of you.' It is George and they both turn and stare at him. 'Ready?' he asks. 'I am,' his daughter replies. They single file up the narrow alleyway to the main road, dressed in T-shirts and shorts, sun glasses set on the tops of their heads, towels and bags over their backs. A woman watches from a doorway, heavily moustached, solid from the legs up. Georgios' wife.

'Did he get rid of the cat?' Julia asks, suspecting the worst. 'It was a condition,' she continues. 'You made a promise.' George hears, and decides to ignore her. 'Well?' They turn into the main street. 'Of course he did,' George says quietly. 'How do you know?' 'Alex or whoever was going to do it. I told you that. They told me.' He strides onwards, past the ranks of mattresses and snorkels, the beach balls and the postcards, and fat Spyros, already sitting in front of his bar, a large black coffee on the small table beside him. And so to the harbour where the Argos, a thirty five foot, twenty year old vessel, awaits them.

Nine o'clock in the morning. It is already twenty three degrees. The sky is untouched by cloud, and as The Argos pulls out of the harbour, past the great breasted bulk of Aphrodite and into the clear waters of the upper Argolic Bay, Tiryns stretches out magnificently quiet, white in the morning. Beyond them, on the horizon, Spetses, and still invisible, Hydra.

The Moores are on the top deck, a move designed by Julia to keep them as far as possible from the bar. 'He's here,' George says, nudging his wife. It is Stavros, the young man. 'Yes, I saw him.' And Gail is with him, she notices. Planned, of course. Scheming little bitch. 'Natural enough, I suppose,' he says, yawning. 'No, it isn't,' she replies, and surprises herself at the intensity of the denial. George fends off the unreasonableness, certain that it will go away as the day progresses. 'Anyway,' he says, 'it's a boat trip. Nothing can happen on a boat trip.'

'I don't want to argue with you, George.'

'Great. Let's have a nice day.'

The Bullocks have come along. Jo is quiet, but acknowledges their presence with a slight wave of his hand. He sits back tightly against the rails, a large straw hat miraculously surviving the breeze. 'Morning. Feel OK?' George shouts out cheerily. Jo nods, and says he is fine. Mary Bullock does not acknowledge them, but hides behind a huge sun hat, dark glasses, and a book. Martin and Maeve are there too. Maeve greets them warmly, coming round from the other side of the boat. 'Hullo.' Her hands light on Tom's head. He squirms. 'Didn't know if you'd be here,' she continues. 'Oh, no, this was a must,' Julia surprises herself by saying, surprising herself even further by the feeling of warmth, companionship, and the need to reciprocate. Maeve turns her attention to George, and says 'And how's George this morning?'

'Oh fine,' Julia intervenes. 'When he got in last night he wasn't, were you, darling? But now he's just fine. George has got great powers of recovery.

That's where his power is, really, isn't it, darling?'

'Anyway,' Maeve purrs, 'Martin was hoping you two would come along. Never know who you're going to come across on these holidays.'

'Fancy a drink?' Martin says, bringing out a bottle of gin from a wicker basket. 'Bit early,' George says hesitantly.

'Hasn't stopped you before,' he hears Julia, reminding him. Which does surprise him, because as they'd got on board she'd herded them all up to the top deck, and he'd known damn well why, of course. Because the bar was on the deck below. Yet now here she was actually encouraging him. So he smiles back at her, and agrees. Yes, he's glad they're here, otherwise it would have been Jo Bullock, who might, for all he knows be alright in the end. Or, he acknowledges the possibility, Mo Greenbaum, the reporter he'd met last night in Yannis' bar. Mo, slightly stooped, thickly moustached, his head ringed with tufts of thick black and greying curls. Mo sits on the bench opposite him, and indicates he is not alone by pointing out the woman sitting beside him. His mouth moves, enunciating clearly, silently, 'Bonkers.'

George nods and remembers. The previous night he'd gone into Yannis'. Julia had feigned boredom and he'd gone out, with a slight nagging pain in his stomach that acted as a general warning to start with, but which later had settled into a dull, almost pleasant tenseness. He'd felt an unfamiliar lilt as he had walked down the middle of the road and through the stream of cars and crowds of half-dressed people; the air was thick with smell, the town unashamedly inviting. Mo had been sitting alone at the bar. Yannis' is set half way down the main street, built showily of wood, with bottles lined from one end to the other. Yannis himself, a bull of a man, brusque and friendly to those he likes, was in the corner, picking his teeth. Mo sat on a stool, wearing a Hawaiian shirt, his large fleshy backside thrust out over the edge.

'My wife is bonkers,' he'd confided, then added, 'though she wasn't when I married her.'

Now, as the Argos sways and pitches into a sudden gust, Martin nods across the deck towards the journalist and says, 'Funny little guy. Gets everywhere. Own private Diaspora.'

'Martin's really a reactionary,' Maeve says. 'He pretends not to be, of course. Not PC. Ever so caring and sharing, but really, underneath, a bit of a shit.'

'I'm not reactionary,' Martin protests. 'I was merely making an observation, and observations relate to truth, facts. Observations aren't reactionary. Only opinions are reactionary.'

'You know him?' George says, surprised, even impressed. 'He told me he's a journalist.'

'That's what he tells himself,' Martin replies. Martin pours gin and tonic carefully, then provides lemon and ice. 'So,' he continues, referring to Mo, 'you've obviously met him before.'

'At Yannis'.' They talk about the location of the bar, and agree. Only George has been inside, and they agree on that. Julia and Maeve listen and share glances, smile, drink gin and tonic. 'Of course, I am not anti-Jewish,' Martin asserts. The comment cleans the air, and the Argos speeds southwards. Half an hour later they anchor offshore and the captain, an otherwise quiet, taciturn figure in black and gold uniform, invites them all to swim.

'Swim!' he shouts. 'Enjoy. Twenty minutes. OK?' He claps his hands, ushering them into the water where, one by one, some tentatively, some at a rush, many of them go.

And it is now that it happens. Julia sits at the railings, watching Maeve and Martin and another figure, who can only be George, strike out like mad dogs towards the shore, some fifty metres away. The sun is now quite high. There is a shadow across the top deck, moving slightly as the tarpaulin itself lifts up and down in the light breeze. Looking down to the deck below she hears

Gail and Stavros, laughing. Then a flash. It is her daughter, a dolphin arching out into the sea below. And she is followed by Stavros, who moves up from the side of the boat in a high arc, then seems to hover.

He is naked.

Julia watches, stunned. The body is frozen, deeply lined by muscle, and heavily matted with hair across the chest. Inch by inch he slides down towards the water, slipping into it finally without effort, without a ripple.

But when he comes to the surface he is all energy, a different being completely, laughing, and certainly by no means naked. Julia catches her breath, and turns to see who might have been watching her. The Greenbaum woman, half naked herself, is poised with a day old copy of The Times, her large breasts reaching towards her gnarled stomach. She is ready to approach. Julia rushes to the lower deck, but the

image of Stavros' naked body pursues her. My God, why had that happened? 'A drink,' she says, once at the bar. 'OK. What you drink? Gincampariwhiskyvodka? maybe the lady drinks a beer?' She is silent, in panic. The barman is a small man whose insolent knowing smile is heavy with meanings she does not care about.

'Gin,' she says. 'No, vodka.'

'OK, the lady drinks a vodka. Tonic?'

'A double vodka. Lemon. No ice.'

'I have no ice.' He is deliberate, and watches her as she takes it from him and drinks.

Why? You're being very silly, Julia, and let's add, a little hysterical. An aberration, that's what it was. An untypical, abnormal nothing, a problem with the light, perhaps. She stares down into the empty glass and remembers a familiar voice saying, 'Julia darling, do come and write that letter over here, next to the light.' That bastard, Lawrence Brown has followed her across here, all those hundreds of bloody miles. Bastard, fat, lecherous, oversexed creep, castration wouldn't be good enough. But Stavros is a young man.

'Are you alright, dear?' It is the Greenbaum woman. Her voice is unexpectedly warm. Julia nods, looks at her, and sees an attentive face, a smile. 'It's just that you seem a little worried, anxious.' The voice drops. And then an apology. 'I know it's an intrusion.'

Julia examines her empty glass. 'I'll have another,' she says, and listens as the returning swimmers clamber up the ladder outside the boat. Maeve, wet, quite beautiful. But how odd her man is, round, small bottom, large belly and very little else.

'It's just that you said "bastard",' the

Greenbaum woman says, explaining.

'Oh, my God, did I?'

'Yes, twice. You were quite passionate, really. Oh, don't get me wrong, I don't have anything against passion. Personally, I long for it, though probably not so much with dear Mo.'

Julia stares at her. Dear God, say something. 'Your husband is a journalist,' she pronounces quietly.

'And your husband is a headmaster,' the older woman replies, which eases things, and Julia laughs. Then the older woman adds, 'Actually, my husband is more a nasty
little scribbler than a journalist, to be honest. As a human being he's alright, I do have to say that. After all I did marry him.'

Julia is not sure of this conversation. Does she now have to say things about George? And did the Greenbaum woman see Stavros, naked in the sunlight?

'Hi, Mum.'

'Hello, darling.'

Tom sidles up to her and puts his nose inches away from Mrs Greenbaum's breasts. Julia throws her arm round him, trying to draw him back. Tom stands resolute, then tries to edge closer. They battle secretly. 'My son,' Julia says. 'Tom.'

'Hello, Tom.'

111

I know what's going on, Julia tells herself, but Tom doesn't know that I know. Just wait till we get home. I'll kill the little bugger. 'This is Mrs Greenbaum,' Julia hisses.

'Hi, Mrs Greenbaum, do you like crabs?' He holds up a four inch crawling mass of legs and pincers, waving it within striking distance of those massive soft glands.

'My,' Mrs Greenbaum says, voice growing sudden strength. 'What a big fellow.'

'Sure is. Gets mad too.'

The crab senses flesh and strikes, but Mrs Greenbaum is faster. She moves back, a graceful movement, hardly seen. At the same time young Tom's face creases in anguish as a foot strikes out and catches him on the shin. 'I used to collect them. Once,' she sings out. 'When I was young, of course.' Her words are addressed to Tom, whose face now shows a small trickle of tears. Julia is not sure exactly what has happened but notices that the crab has disappeared, that Tom is unhappy, and that the Greenbaum woman's face is lit up with more than a trace of a smile. 'Of course, not now. Mo wouldn't like it.' She sighs. 'And now, I think I'll have a drink. Barman? Double scotch. And make that a big one. Straight.'

The engines start, and the Argos moves off.

'That old cow kicked me,' Tom whispers to his

mother.

'She is not an old cow,' Julia says comforting him, and disputing only one half of the observation.

Hydra is full of rather expensive yachts.

Jo Bullock and family, Martin and Maeve, the Moore family and the Greenbaums sit in the shade at an outdoor cafe overlooking the very busy harbour. Julia is still edgy. Stavros and Gail are in the shops.

'It is definitely not right for a young girl of fifteen to spend so much time with a man. Stavros is not a boy,' Julia says to George. 'He's a young man. And maybe not so young, either.' The image of that diving, naked body haunts her. George doesn't reply and she says, 'George, I want you to talk to her. We've been here three days and she hasn't been away from him. What do you think he wants, eh?' She nudges him, and he retreats from her, saying warningly, 'Don't do that, Julia.' He smiles at Maeve, who watches closely, but doesn't hear them. George finally says, 'Maybe he wants to practise his English.'

'Oh, for Christ's sake! I don't want her to get pregnant.'

'She won't.'

'Oh, yes? Did he promise you?'

Mo's wife is now mercifully clothed and Julia nods at her. 'Earnest conversations with one's husband on holiday, my dear,' she says, leaning across the table towards Julia, 'are not good for one. Or you.' Mo Greenbaum hears, and catches George's eye. His fingers shoot out in the direction of his wife, discreetly. Bonkers. His lips move. Maeve explains to Mo that she has been to Hydra before, and he says that the same is true for him. 'So,' he summarises, 'we've both written articles about the bloody island. Mine was awful.'

'It was worse than that,' his wife says.

'It was terrible,' he allows. He smiles at Maeve and his voice is syrup, 'But I expect yours was brilliant. Who did it? Harpers? Vogue? Sunday Times Mag? You do look the sort. Sarah, doesn't she look the sort?'

'Sunday Times,' Jo Bullock interrupts with great intensity. He looks from one to the other, puppydog eyes full, blooded slightly, fleshy cheeks, and he leans on the table, eyeing them both, and his voice is larded, 'I remember it.'

'You don't read The Sunday Times,' his wife says snappily. It is the first time anyone has heard her speak. Mary Bullock is the sudden but brief centre of attention.

She hides behind a newspaper.

Nothing more can be said on the matter, but everyone knows that a knife has been drawn.

Hydra ignores them, and burns under the growing heat.

But it is now known that the Greenbaum woman is called Sarah.

What is it, Julia finds herself wondering, about the Bullocks? Is he that bad, that boring? Is he just lonely? Does he love his wife? Could anyone love his wife? She stares at Mary Bullock's paper, the paper held up in front of her face like a wall. The Guardian. Aptly named, she notes, and ironically it tells her nothing. Julia registers and accepts the fascination for the woman behind it. There are children. There is marriage. Was there ever any passion? And she thinks then of George, and her own children, and tells herself that passion is really just a word.

The Bullock children are, as usual, quiet. The boy reads a comic, and his sister looks at a cat that has sneaked up beside her. Very gently, in silence, without comment, her hand drops. The cat moves towards it, and rubs gently. The girl smiles, and her eyes light up, then close as the smile is drawn in carefully. The cat strays, the hand lingers, the smile too.

Julia decides to move. 'How old are you?' she asks the girl, who looks up, startled, and retrieves her hand.

'She's eleven,' her brother answers, and Julia turns her attention towards him and sees a very thin faced child, with the kind of skin she'd always thought of as sickly white. Young Tom would spit at him, yet there is very little difference in their ages.

Their mother is undoubtedly aware of this approach, and Jo too, who smiles at her. Is that encouragement, she wonders?

Sarah Greenbaum and Julia turn towards each other, and between them there is a brief moment of a secret shared. Julia gathers strength. 'Are you having fun?' she asks the boy.

'Oh, yes. Lots.' He is dressed in shorts and a white shirt. And the girl? She wears a gingham dress. Green. And white socks.

There is a strain now, unspoken, that Julia feels tightening across the table between herself and these quiet children and their parents. 'Come, dear.' She feels Sarah Greenbaum's hand on her arm. 'Let's go gawk at those carpets and the gold.'

George agrees to go in search of cats. It is Maeve's idea. Maeve is a cat and he follows her. Lithe, angular, aloof, and yet warm. 'I want to go look at cats,' she had commanded. Martin rolls his eyes upwards but gets to his feet. George has the impression that he always falls in line with his wife, following, and then walking beside her, a still youngish man whose size and weight will be easier on him in another fifteen years.

'Come on, George, you too,' Maeve says.

'So,' Maeve says, as they move away from the square, 'it is Sarah. Mo and Sarah.'

'Wish she'd wear more clothes,' Martin says. He is all in white, long white trousers and a Lacoste tennis shirt, his stomach straining behind the belt.

'Awful,' Maeve agrees.

George walks beside her, and wonders about her breasts. She sees him looking, and laughs. He thinks words, silently daring her to catch them. 'I'm thinking about your breasts.' He paints the words on the narrow cobbled street, and she walks across them, long legged. 'Is he famous?' George asks, 'Mo, I mean?'

'Mo Greenbaum?' It is Maeve who answers. 'Oh, he's written this and that.'

'Are you famous?' George makes love to her.

'No.'

'I've seen you on TV.'

But Maeve rejects the gambit in favour of a cat. 'Look,' she says, 'it's a black one.' They have turned off the main square that faces the harbour and are now climbing. The island rises steeply around them. Narrow stepped streets, white houses edged in blue and green, tightly packed together.

A black cat stands in a doorway, back arched.

'Here, puss, puss.' Maeve bends towards the cat. George stares at her backside, tight inside the yellow slacks. 'Just what is it about Greece and cats?' Maeve wonders aloud.

'Christ knows,' Martin says, his voice pained, tired, telling. George grins and sympathises. 'We've got a dead one under our villa. On the beach,' he says. Of course, he had lied to Julia. It was a lie. Nothing was going to be done about that cat. Nothing.

Martin grimaces, but Maeve is interested. 'Really? I mean, is it really dead?'

'Oh, yes, rotting. Probably.' George is philosophical. 'Julia asked me to get someone to get rid of it.'

'Well?'

'Well, he said he would but he didn't.'

'Christ, it's bloody hot,' Martin says wearily. 'Mind you, Greeks are like that,' he adds, referring back to George's comment. 'What in the hell are we doing up here, anyway? Can't we go back and have a beer?'

'Shhh!' Maeve points upwards. A white and grey tom lies on the rounded top of a white painted stone wall. 'He's watching us. Puss. Puss. What is he thinking?'

'He thinks we're bloody daft,' Martin replies.

The cat yawns.

'What do you do?' George asks Martin. 'I thought you sold BMWs.'

'Martin's a European,' Maeve says. 'And he tells other people how to think, act, do, be. Don't you, darling?'

George regrets asking the question. 'Look,' he says, 'there's a black one.'

They stop and examine the cat in the small alleyway to the right. 'It's the same one,' Martin pronounces. But Maeve disagrees. 'No, it's not. It's different.'

George can't see any difference. He wonders about Martin and Maeve together. Sex with Maeve. Does he start it, or does she? He does. No, it would be her.

'What are you thinking, George?' Maeve puts her arm through his and George reflects that he is with another woman and that Julia, his wife, is off somewhere else.

'Oh, nothing. About work, actually. Some new desks I've had to order. Junior classes, you know. They attack them, the kids, worse than woodworm.'

'Rubbish.' Her eyes widen.

They walk close together, the three of them. Martin swipes at a cat with a long stick. The cat screams, and scuttles round a corner.

'Look,' Maeve whispers, 'there's Jo.' They see him, standing alone, peering into a shop window. Maeve leans into George, and says, 'Let's follow him.'

They stop at Spetses. Mo and Sarah Greenbaum decide to stay on board. Mo is pale and sits back against the railings with hands clasped in front of his belly.

'Off you go, dears,' Sarah says to the rest. 'Mo's a bit squeamish.'

'Bit too much up and down,' Jo says, grinning. He makes waves with his hands.

'Don't stand there, dear,' Sarah warns him. 'He might throw up over you.'

Jo walks off the boat and onto the stone jetty, followed by his wife and two children.
'Why do Jews look so Jewish?' he observes to his wife as they walk slowly up from the harbour to the town. Mary Bullock, if she knows the answer, does not tell him.

'Bloody awful place,' Mo says with a certain tiredness, nodding towards the dull town on the island. 'Wrote about it once for The Telegraph. It was such a bloody boring subject the buggers wouldn't print it.'

Sarah remembers.

'Why do you think they're here?' Mo says, pointing at the small white shape walking just paces behind the strident yellow of his wife. Sarah goes to the railings, nods, and clears her throat. 'Slumming. This isn't their scene. Should be in Barbados. Goa. She's up to something.'

'Don't trust her,' Mo says.

'Observation or instruction?' his wife queries.

'Both. Christ, I feel sick. Why did we come on this bloody awful holiday?'

'God knows. You said you wanted to.'

'Well,' Mo sighs. Then says, voice rising, ' Why can't they bloody cook, these people? All that bloody grease and the bloody tomatoes, and the sodding lamb. Why isn't there any decent fish, for Christ's sake?'

'You shouldn't speak like that,' she cautions with clear disapproval.

'I'm going to be sick,' he announces.

'Well, go to the other side, where you can't be seen.'

Mo heaves himself to his feet and joins her at the railings. 'The other side,' she hisses.

'Can't. Sorry.' He throws up noisily into the water.

Sarah looks up. Not thirty metres away she sees the three young men standing in the water, all of them drinking beer from cans. Behind them, on the beach she recognises another group - the Preston lady and her two boys.

Mo is the centre of attention for them all. He heaves again, rejecting churned up tomato and onion and small unchewable messes of lamb. He pants loudly on the railings.

'Well done, Mo,' Sarah says cheerily, smiling at an astonished and evidently very embarrassed Ann Preston, who sits on the beach, topless, legs up to cover her breasts. Trying to escape attention the embarrassed mother turns away and looks towards the town, which she cannot see because the small spit of sand is surrounded
by concrete walls. Her boys stand at the water's edge, wearing flippers, goggles over their eyes, snorkels rearing from their heads.

Then one of the three young men finally finds voice. 'Do it again!' he yells. 'Do it again!' the three chant in unison.

'Tell them to fuck off,' Mo begs, gesturing to his wife.

'Fuck off!' she bravely shouts back. Which silences the three, who stand motionless for a while in the water, then turn to each other, drink, mumble, and walk back to the shore. A beer can is hurled against the concrete wall, followed by two more. Sarah waves at the woman on the beach. A hand is raised in return. The two children drift just a few metres from the boat.

'Ugh!' One of the boys rears out of the water. The other surfaces, then dives deeply. Sarah and Mo watch as the remaining child flees from the drifting evidence of Mo's lunch.

'I did say the other side,' Sarah rebukes Mo quietly. Sarah continues to stand at the railings. The three young men are now lying just a short distance from Ann Preston. Their bodies are burnt red. One of them wears a plaster on his nose. Another has a bandage round one knee. They are drinking again, beer cans lifting mechanically up and down.

'Why is she slumming here?' Sarah wonders aloud. 'Maeve, I mean.'

'Working on something, I expect,' Mo says. 'Another bloody article. Or a book.'

'A book?'

'Yes, why not?' he says wearily.

'What? Fiction? She can't write fiction.' Sarah is adamant.

Mo stares unhappily around him. 'It's all so bloody obvious, isn't it? The sun. The sea. All this bloody light. Greece isn't meant to be written about. It's meant to be photographed.'

'You're a real prat, Mo Greenbaum,' his wife replies. 'What about the Durrells? What about Homer?"

'Oh, sod the Durrells.' He belches, then says reflectively, 'I feel better now.'

'It's the people, Mo. That's what she's writing about. And that makes him think. 'You and me?' he asks. 'Uh, uh, maybe and those Moores, perhaps, that perfect English couple.'

'Are they?'

'All could have beens and would have been ifs. Unlike the Jews, or the Americans.'

'Christ,' his voice snaps, 'I wish you wouldn't.'

And she laughs inwardly, taunting him.

The boat heaves and Mo grips the railings. They all realise immediately what is happening. A large fishing vessel moored the other side of the Argos has started up and is already moving out into the harbour, prior to leaving for the open sea. As it moves, the water in the small enclosed harbour area is thrust violently outwards. The Argos lifts, rocks and bangs against the jetty, and huge waves roll swiftly across the few metres towards the beach.

Mo and Sarah witness seconds of calm before bedlam.

The three young men are now sitting, beer cans raised, next to three large bags with **IBIZA** written in bright red across them. Just a little way from them Ann Preston is blithely applying suntan lotion to her breasts. Her boys are splashing water.

'Shit!'

The young men leap to their feet and retreat to the wall, where the water bubbles around their legs. Ann Preston's boys disappear, but emerge seconds later only a little way from the Argos. Their mother has moved quickly, gathering a towel to her breasts, and reaching for her handbag as the water strikes. She topples backwards, but miraculously regains her feet. Other towels, a book, a magazine, float out to sea on the retreating water.

Her boys splutter back to her, and she harangues them. 'Damn you!' she shouts at the youngest son. Goggles on his hair, shivering beside the soggy remains of a newspaper, he protests his innocence. 'I didn't do anything!'

'Well, don't just stand there.' She is angry, and helpless. Her two boys go in search of lost possessions; she clutches a sodden dress. The rest of the group drift back from the town, and all of them, including the Prestons, and the three young men, finally clamber back on board.

The captain greets them, smiling, a professional who has been through this routine a hundred times and more.

TUESDAY

Cats.

Tiryns is full of cats. They wander, dead spirits, never really full bodied healthy cats, but living dead cats, with inquisitional eyes and lean hungry forms. Cats of Greece adorn the postcards, and walk across the roofs. They steal under chairs, and wait.

Maeve is a cat, a large knowledgeable cat. What would Lawrence Brown make of her? She'd scratch his eyes out, and so should I.

We went to Hydra, and I have now met and like the Greenbaum woman, whose name is Sarah. It was, I suppose, an ordinary sea trip. Nothing unusual happened, except that Mo got sick. At lunch we all sat together. The Bullocks, the Greenbaums, us. Stavros was there, with Gail. He is a nice young man. I have to say that I feel a little in two minds about the three young men who keep cropping up everywhere; it as though they are playing a part, and that they can't be as stupid as they look. I feel too that I should say something about the Bullocks, but am at a total loss. I've thought about it, and there really seems nothing to say. Perhaps I'm tired.

This ouzo is disgusting. I'd never drink it at home.

Ann Preston is above me. Why does she fascinate me so much? Maybe it's her silence. I watched her tonight walking down the beach. Where had she been? Quite tall, and though not thin by any means, rather angular. Handsome, rather than beautiful. Her face is alive; it must be the eyes. There is something about her which disturbs me, too. I don't think I could look at her long, nor have her look at me. There would be too much that suddenly seemed to need saying. But I wouldn't be able. Every now and again her chair shifts, and I can hear papers turning, and a glass every now and again lifted, then once more set down on the table. We are both on our balconies, both facing out towards the bay. Coronisi is still alight, but it is not late. The bars are open and there are people on the beach, walking. George has gone out for a drink, thank God. I don't give a damn who with, or where. But I am angry with George and his male arrogance, and the male stupidity in him, and the way he makes me think of that bastard at home in his, my office, Lawrence bloody Brown in his stained and overlarge brown suit, sneering at me from behind his desk in the corner.

Really, it was the cat that made me mad. When

we got back from the boat trip, Tom started it all by saying, 'Hey, Dad, that cat stinks.' George and I were in the bathroom, peeling off clothes.

'Shut up!' George said sharply.

'I thought you'd arranged something, everything, at least that's what you promised me, George.' I knew I was going to snap. 'You promised.'

'I did.'

'So?'

'This is not England.'

'Do not make specious comparisons, damn you.' I remember my voice, cutting. Bastard. Tom was in the doorway. 'What's specious?' he asked.

'Where's your sister?' George intervened, ever a master at diversion.

'Do not bring your daughter into this.'

'Why not? You do. Always.'

'Actually, George. Actually, it's the cat,' I said, close to screaming.

'And it sure stinks,' Tom butted in, still standing in the doorway, baseball cap on his head, T-shirt scarred with ice cream.

'Where's Gail?' I asked him.

'With that guy.'

'Oh, Christ,' I replied. The fear, the worry, had slipped out involuntarily, and George leered at me. 'George, this is very simple. Get rid of the cat or I go to The Delphi.' He considered this, as did I.

We don't have the money, but money makes George consider all things.

He grunted, and said I was right. Which I was. Bloody little Tom asked if he could help. 'What about dinner?' I asked. It always seems to be me who has to ask the obvious.

We agreed to meet at The Ship at nine thirty. I showered, went out for a walk on my own, and then had a drink.

We all met at The Ship at nine thirty. Gail was there, on time, dressed in tight jeans and a top that hung around her breasts like string. I asked about the cat, and George nodded, and said, 'It's OK.' I eyed Tom, who nodded at me. 'Well,' I said, avoiding the lie, 'thank God for that.'

When we got back to the house I knew that something was different, though what exactly it took me quite a while to work out. It wasn't until I went out onto the beach and saw something dark and solid about the lower part of the villa that I realised what it was. Examining it, I could see that someone, or even several people, had bricked up the hole where the cat had been with cement and breeze blocks.

George stood behind me, watching, a shadow in the shadows.

'You know about this, George?'

He grunted. 'You wanted me to fix it.'

'Who? Who did it?' I demanded.

'Georgios. It's his villa. Georgios has a supply of breeze blocks.' George also went on to explain that Georgios owned villas all over the Peloponnese. His geography surprised me. 'What about the cat?' I asked.

George appeared to have lost all memory of the cat. 'Where's the cat, George? Did he get rid of the cat?'

'Well, I expect so. Of course he did. I asked him, didn't I? Of course he got rid of the bloody cat, Jesus Christ, who do you think I am?'

I knew then that he was lying, George and Georgios, both of them. They hadn't got rid of the bloody cat. They'd incarcerated it.

So I told George what I thought of him, which wasn't much, and he said that if I felt like that he was going out for a drink, and I told him to sod off and that I didn't care if he got raped, and he said he wished he would, which is so bloody typical and so bloody puerile. If I could get at that cat I'd stuff it down his throat.

FOUR

At the age of twenty Andreas had gone to London. Accurate records of what he did in the two years that he was there do not exist. There are occasional anecdotes, released every now and again to one or other of his relations in Athens or even at times to Fat Spyros or Kostas, the fisherman. Generally, however, that period of his life is hidden from public view. The same is true of the time he spent in France at the end of the sixties, the months he spent in Rome, and the exile in New York. Andreas' life away from Tiryns is hidden in darkness, with only the odd murmur and rumour to relieve it. When he had gone to England he had left with little more than a prayer and a handful of drachmas. Now, he is one of the wealthier men in Tiryns, owner of Minoa Travel, a rather quiet but imposing figure, and always dressed better than anyone else.

Today he celebrates his birthday alone, not because he has to - there is hardly a man or woman in the place who wouldn't come running to him if he just so much as looked - but because that is what he wants. His humour tends to self-absorption and he has what his wife calls moods.

She is a quiet woman who spends much of her time in Athens. From time to time she becomes pregnant. The children stay in Athens, and are only brought down to the beach in the summer when the father has the mind to call them. No one, not even Fat Spyros, asks after Andreas' wife. Few, apart from Stavros, her young brother-in-law, even think of her by her name, Margarita.

It is five o'clock, and there is a dull stillness in the air. Andreas sits alone in the open doorway of his villa. Down on the beach the wind blows, and the water swells up and down against the harbour walls. It is an uncertain time of day, not right for beer, or coffee, or ouzo.

Hibiscus runs red down the thick hedge that grows up against the concrete wall around the villa. The Mercedes stands in the shadows of the carport. A clock in the large open room that forms the greater part of the lower floor of the villa counts the seconds. Maria, the girl who does the washing and cooking, enters the house through a side door. Andreas sits in his doorway and drinks coffee. He feels an overbearing sense of melancholy that is largely self-induced, and partly a product of the still, noiseless, place in which he lives. He asks her for ouzo, and she brings it to him without a word, the bottle on a wooden tray, the glass accompanied by a carafe of water and a bowl of pistachio nuts.

On his twenty first birthday he had gone to stay as a paying guest in the house of Dolly Person. Dolly Person taught him a lot about England. She was an elderly lady who lived alone, apart from a younger brother called Robert, a thin, coughing man in a red woollen cardigan, quiet, who had never known much about the real world, having spent most of his life with his sister. 'England,' Dolly would say to Andreas, 'must be so difficult for a young man like you to understand.' And Robert, sitting in a small worn armchair would nod, and rub his long heavily veined nose and say, 'Well, of course, it is. The lad's a foreigner.'

'You mustn't mind Bob,' Dolly would tell him.

In London Andreas worked in kitchens and hotels. He earned enough money to travel, and he decided that in life he would make money. He ignored the insults and endless comparisons that living in London forced him to accept as part of his daily life. A Greek living in a city which had once been great and was now showing every sign of decay was, without friends and any influence, in no position to do anything but maintain silence.

Dolly Person and her brother grew to depend on him. They loved him like a dog.

One bright Saturday morning she took him to Bloomsbury. Andreas pretended amazement and followed her gaze, her excited indications of old houses once occupied by the great. Outside the British Museum he pretended ignorance. 'When you go back to Greece, Andreas,' she'd said, standing next to him, buttoned up in an old brown coat and a bright red beret perched on her head, 'I want you to remember what you've seen here.'

He did not tell her that he knew the museum like an old friend.

She took him to see the marbles. 'The Elgin Marbles,' she purred. 'Now, that's culture. Such a great man.'

'I didn't know Elgin was Greek,' he said, suddenly overcome by anger.

'Well, of course he wasn't. He was British. Greek! Good Heavens!' Dolly was genuinely outraged and strode off into the middle of the room.

Now, in the heat of the day the memory of that small, confused, ignorant, but very kind English lady returns to him and haunts him over the ouzo. He rubs his face and stares outside. He watches a smallish, round faced man, well overweight, walk painfully past him up the hill, and a little later he recognises the figure as Martin Rushton. Andreas grins and rises to his feet. Quietly, he moves out into his patio and watches the Englishman's backside swinging to and fro in the overtight nylon shorts. He raises his glass at the departing figure. He has always tried to keep track of who his guests are and he has heard that Rushton and his wife had made a name for themselves over the years. He savours the ouzo. It is sweet, and he reaches for more water. Why do the British, who are islanders, pretend that they can be continental? They can't. It is an argument he had heard from a French traveller in California. The Frenchman had been passionate, consumed, and declared loudly that the British would never make good Europeans, at which a lone British expatriate standing a couple of metres away along the bar had sneered and said, 'Why in the fuck would we want to be good Europeans, anyway? All those bloody French and bloody Germans. Fuck them.'

Last year Andreas had received a short letter from Bob Person to say that his sister had died. 'Thought you might like to know,' the letter had said. 'She always did have a soft spot for you.'

Andreas thinks of his English guests, the Moores, the Prestons, the men, the women, the children, and then he looks out at the sky and finds that the light is very clear, and still, and that the afternoon is suspended around him on great pillars of silence.

A lizard runs across the wall, fast. That and the smell of pine needles bring back another place, far to the west, on the Atlantic coast. Estoril. Thirty years ago.

Ann Preston stands quite still, like the lizard, poised. Its head is turned to one side, small eyes raised to the sun, long fingers splayed, gripping the rockface. She remembers another lizard, clinging to its own rock, with the wind coming in from the Atlantic, and the clouds thundering up from Cascais and beyond, and the pine needles, as now, confused in shadow and light.

A car passes, too quickly, breaking through the unexpected fusion of memory and the very real light and heat of the afternoon. Her children are snorkelling. They are strong boys, independent. Her hands are deep in the pockets of her long summer dress. Flowers, red and blue, crawl over a wall from a garden to the left and hang towards her. She's always been useless at names, trees, flowers, animals. The entire plant and animal kingdom is somehow made that more unknowable by her inability to remember names. Her husband, Geoff, had always mocked her for that. How can you not know what a plane tree is? Look. A plane tree. And so with hibiscus, gardenia, the great crested grebe, Alium ursinum and the humble coot. But Geoff always knew, his mind a vast warehouse of neatly ordered facts, plants, trees, animal life, classified by name and number, colour and species, as indeed he had classified her. Preston. Ann. Wife.

Of course, she could have taken his anger, his obvious disdain, more easily if only he'd shown more of it, been more recognisably disdainful. Anyway, Geoff has gone, is gone, and she is now declassified. The boys had accepted the departure, visit him once a month in Lewes, and rarely mention him. They are careful not to hurt her, not to raise his name, nor bring his things, the books, old clothes, the tennis rackets, anywhere near her. Strange solicitation, she has often thought, when the two of them make her life such hell in so many other ways.

Money isn't easy. Can she blame them for not understanding everything? They are still almost children. They don't understand that she doesn't have the money. And Tiryns this year was only possible because of Dorothy dying. She starts off down the alleyway, white villas climbing up to left and right, adorned with traditional blue and green doors and shutters, and not so traditional TV antennae, and wonders just how many holidays, how many half-naked bathers on the beach, are this year sponsored by the gift of recently dead relations.

Poor old Dot, dying alone in that bloody awful room.

She stops, and looks about her, surprised. She is in an open courtyard, and there in the window is that young man, the woman's friend, standing with his hands in his pockets, his upper body quite bare, his head resting against the glass. She has invaded, and is deeply conscious of having done so. But there are other stirrings. The woman and this young man have fascinated her from the beginning, more than any of the others. And she knows what it is, not just the difference in age, although that is part of it. It is more the silent knowingness of the relationship, the way they are so totally quiet. She has felt this need to watch them become a compulsion, and only yesterday found herself walking behind them on the beach, measuring the distance between their bodies, recognising the seemingly coordinated swing of their arms and legs as they picked their way among the sleepers, and the readers, the bodies on the sand.

It is years now since she has been in love. It was after she and Geoff had been married for seven years, in Italy. An American who'd stayed in the same hotel. Geoff hadn't suspected, as she was after all Preston, Ann, wife, and not Ann the lover, the adulterer. It had only lasted three days, but she had been in love. Now she stands

quite still, glancing from time to time at the face of
the young man, half-scared that he will wake from
his trance and find her there, watching him. She
edges back out of the courtyard, tense, certain that
if she stays any longer she'll be seen. The alleyway
gives way very quickly into the large vine covered
courtyard of The Golden Moon which still, at this
time of the afternoon is crowded. A table of
Greeks are playing cards. The woman she now
knows to be Julia Moore is talking intensely to her
daughter. A family argument, perhaps? The vine
leaves and the trees move with the wind, and
rustle. Suddenly one of the Greek men jumps up
and rushes down to the beach, waving his arms and
yelling at two small boys at the edge of the water.

She looks around her, feeling a change in the
air. It has gone cold. There are clouds.

It is the wind.

She walks through the courtyard and down to
the beach, and sees the waves whipping up
between the islands. There are still a great many
craft out in the bay, surfboards and pedallos for the
most part, with the small fishing vessels of the
locals either securely anchored or drawn up on the
beach. Only yesterday she had heard someone talk
about this wind. Five o'clock. You could set your
watch by it. She looks at her wrist; it is two
minutes past five.

The same man who had left his friends at the table now rushes past her and up the beach towards her own villa, yelling and again waving his arms. She is aware too of someone beside her, someone she has noticed before. 'There's a man and a woman out on a pedallo,' the Greek says, not facing her, though she knows it is for her. She turns towards him. Last night he had followed her, in the street. He stares at her, eyes held steady, his face full, a boyish face, but lined. 'They've got a young girl with them.'

She knows who he's talking about, and only now the urgency of it strikes her. 'Do you have a boat?' she asks.

He shrugs his shoulders, looks down, and says 'OK. Come with me.' She walks beside him. Of course, she knew he had a boat. Walking up and down all day by herself, sometimes just sitting, seeing things, knowledge creeps inside, and waits.

'Why?'

Gail's question does not surprise her mother. What does surprise her is the utter reasonableness of the way in which it is delivered, a quiet but determined interrogative. Julia looks up, lets a swift breath of air pass through her lips and says, 'Well.' Which doesn't really allow her to pass into silence, but she does. The word is more of a comment on her own judgment. 'It's just that I don't think you should spend so much time with him. It's what we both feel. Your father and I.' Lame, Julia. She manages a smile for her daughter, who looks back, and through her. Fifteen years old. Is that a fact which is even relevant? Her daughter. A woman. A child. 'I want you to be careful,' she says.

'I know you do. I am.'

'You are?'

'Yes.'

'Then...?'

'Please, Mum. I'm grown up.'

'You're fifteen years old. Fifteen is not grown up. What about Aids?'

'He hasn't got Aids.'

'I'm not saying he has.'

'Then why bring it up?'

'Because I'm your mother and I care.'

'I care, too. Christ, it's my body.'

'Don't say, 'Christ'.'

'OK. But it's still my body. I know about Aids. I can read, you know.'

'You don't get Aids from reading.'

They fall silent, and Gail lights a cigarette.

'Oh, for God's sake, Gail. Don't smoke. You know I hate it. Does he wear a condom?'

'I don't know.'

'What! For God's sake, girl, you must know.'

'Mother, don't raise your voice. Please.'

'You're damn right I'll raise my voice. You said you know about Aids but you can't even tell me if he uses a condom!'

'I said I don't know.' Gail is quiet, and reasonable. 'We don't, you know, do it.' The reply is accompanied by another silence, during which Ann Preston walks into the courtyard. Mother and daughter turn, taking advantage of the appearance of someone familiar.

'I'm sorry,' Julia says quietly. Is her daughter smiling? The suggestion that she might be lying, however, is given no time to develop because Petros, Georgios' second son, suddenly leaves his table and runs onto the beach, yelling.

'I think the couple with that girl are out there,' Gail says.

'Who? Oh, that couple. Where's Tom?' But Tom is OK. He comes up the beach with Nicos beside him, an octopus writhing in his right hand. 'Mum? Can I cook this?'

Ann Preston follows the Greek out to The Ship, and then round the broken down concrete quay where his boat pulls at its ropes.

'Get in,' he tells her.

She wades into the water, watches while he

clambers up over the side, and grabs his outstretched hand when he reaches down for her.

She falls into the boat.

It is hard pulling round the end of the quay and she wonders for a moment about the boat being able to head out across the water and into the wind, but as they straighten up, with Aphrodite to the right, the engine roars and she has to cling hard to the side. Tiryns slips past to the left, almost hidden in spray. Coronisi comes up on the right, with two slow moving fishing vessels edging out from the side of her as they make their way towards the harbour. It is time, oddly, for reflection. The sky surprises her, slightly clouded, but without apparent danger, but further out, as the bay spreads towards Spetses, the cloud is dark and heavy. The wind is up, and the sea runs strongly, whipping round the boat as it heads out at an angle against the waves. Tiryns drops back still further, the small boats swaying back and forwards against the shoreline, the last of the windsurfers struggling towards the beach, the last of the pedallos thrashing the remaining few metres towards the shore.

Except for Mr Jones and Mrs Hillier, and the young girl.

She'd noticed them first at Gatwick, standing just in front of them in the check-in queue. She remembered wondering what it was on holidays that could make exceedingly ordinary people seem in the most unusual of ways exceedingly odd. Because the couple were ordinary, as was the young girl. Tall, healthy. The man had broad shoulders, was muscular, and good looking in a Quaker Oats sort of way, as was the woman, tall, relaxed, with a quiet, seemingly unmarked, almost pretty face. The girl was in shorts, with a Lanzarote T-shirt, long blonde hair, very quiet. Yet there had been an intensity about the small unit of three, an unusual suggestion of unspoken, perhaps unspeakable possibilities, that singled them out, and had made her look, and notice, and remember. So, when Louise on the coach in from Athens had been calling out the names and the villas, the Bullocks, and the Anstruthers, and the Thomases, and the lot up in the Villa Dora, and then finally Mr Jones and party, and those three had stood up and walked down the coach, it had not surprised her. Following their steps down the coach and down into the side alley behind the post office, she had felt curiosity tug at her. A premonition, perhaps, of this lunatic journey out into the Argolic Bay in this flimsy boat. She glances at the man at the tiller of his boat, and is uneased by his own sense of purpose, the calmness of the set of his jaw, the disinterest in his eyes, and the accent that tells her he has spent time in London. Years, perhaps. She senses her own arrogance, and his, and is distanced from him by the isolation he has created about her, his anger at the stupidity of the man on the pedallo. His face is seaward; he says nothing. He wears a blue and white striped T-shirt, crisp, clean. He pushes against the tiller and indicates the far shore, past Assini. The clouds are heavier than before. 'Where is it?' she asks. 'The pedallo.' He points, down into the bay. She stares at where his finger indicates, and sees nothing, except for the round island of Plataea, empty except for goats and snakes. Tiryns is now no more than a bundled outline of white ragged edges. What kind of fool, she wonders, would bring a pedallo out this far? She feels an involved fascination with what she is doing, the sea, the man just seconds away from her, and the wind that strengthens, and pushes in gusts against the boat.

Two other boats come out from Tiryns. Alexos from The Delphi and Fat Spyros, and it is Spyros who gets there first. They find the pedallo a kilometre the Tiryns side of Plataea. The young girl is crying, the adults are shaking, pale, exhausted. 'Ise enas ilithios!' Spyros shouts, as he pulls the bewildered Englishman into his boat. 'Idiot!'

Ann Preston shares his anger, suddenly overwhelmed. The three boats rock together against the pedallo. The young girl throws up over the side, retching uncontrollably. In Spyros' boat the man and woman sit close to each other, saying nothing, watching the Greeks tie the pedallo behind Alexos' fishing boat. 'OK,' Ann Preston's companion says in English, 'we'll take the girl and the mother back. He,' and he jerks his finger at the Englishman, 'can go with Spyros.' The contempt is leaden.

There follow moments of frantic activity as the young girl and the woman step over into their boat. Ann Preston catches at them as they clamber across. The Greek moves back to the tiller and pulls out a blanket from a recess. Mother and child take it, and huddle close together beneath it. The boat speeds back to the beach, and the wind pushes the water into rolling waves that run quickly across the bay. Ann Preston wonders at the awfulness of not knowing what to say to the woman.

One of the three young men falls from the third floor of The Delphi and lives.

It happens on the evening of the first Thursday, not long after Mr Jones and Mrs Hillier have been rescued from their pedallo, and is perhaps the only event that could have saved the man from the degree of gossip and criticism which many think he rightly deserves. It happens quite without warning. The three young men do not have a room at The Delphi, and Alexos, the manager, is amazed that they were able to gain entry, as on their arrival he has spotted them on the beach and given instructions that they should not be served in the outside bar, and not allowed to enter the body of the hotel.

It is just before seven in the evening and the wind has died down. Mrs Simmons is sitting with a campari soda at a table near the centre of the outside bar, staged inside a very blue Laura Ashley dress that Betty refuses even to comment on, an unread paper- back in her lap. She nibbles at a saucer of pistachios. Betty sits to one side, drinking retsina.

'I don't know how you can drink that stuff, Betty.'

'I don't know,' Betty says, 'I rather like it.'

'It's such awful plonk. It would be banned in France. Probably is.' Harriet's barb makes Betty turn away. She sees Harriet Simmons dressed in that awful thing that would have been atrocious even on someone twenty years younger, and tells herself that the woman is getting on her nerves.

Not the least of it is that Harriet owes her money. Of course, the financial agreement between them has never been clear, but it is now becoming increasingly unworkable. 'One reason I drink retsina,' she says under her breath and in the direction of the sea beyond, 'is that I can't afford campari soda.'

'What was that?' her companion demands stiffly.

'Oh, nothing. Nothing.'

'I thought you said you wanted a campari soda. Well, I'm not stopping you. Get drunk, if that's what you want. Everyone else seems to.'

'What on earth was that?' Betty says, getting up quickly as an uncomfortably familiar peal sounds out from a balcony above the stretched tarpaulin covering the outside bar. She rushes outside onto the beach, where she is soon joined by a growing group of onlookers. The Delphi rises to five floors, and is capped by a flat roof. On the side that faces the sea the three upper floors have five windows, each with a rather narrow balcony; fifteen bedrooms, all with a sea view. The best in the hotel, and some say the best in Tiryns. Harriet Simmons and Betty have a room on the third floor, but on the right side of the building, not facing the beach. At this moment Betty's attention and indeed that of everybody else is focused firmly on the right hand balcony of the third floor, where the three young Englishmen stand drinking retsina from bottles and shouting abuse at two very confused young men on the beach below.

'Go back to Krautland, you fucking Kraut.'

'Yes, sod off, you bloody Nazi. Go back to Germany.'

'I am not from Germany,' one of the two young men responds. Blond, brow-knitted, anxious, Norwegian.

'Then fuck off, anyway.'

'And I am not a Nazi,' retorts the other Norwegian. Both young men are bewildered and angry. 'You're a Nazi. You're a right wing hooligan with too much drinking and too much shouting with bad words. You're supposed to be a European.'

'Fuck Europe.'

The comment is complemented by a moment of silence. To the crowd gathered on the beach the three on the balcony appear to be in discussion. Alexos approaches the two Norwegians and asks if they know how the three had got into the hotel.

'They climbed in?' he says with disbelief.

'Yes,' one of the Norwegians replies. 'With a ladder. Into that room, there.' Betty sees him pointing at the room round the corner of the third floor. Her room. And Harriet's, of course. 'Oh,

Dear God,' she says. 'Dear God.'

'What on earth is it, Betty?' Mrs Simmons demands, strident, cigarette in one hand and her campari in the other. Betty almost dies at the public display of the dress, the entire ensemble. 'Oh, for God's sake, Harriet, do get back inside. Please. Now. Back.' She waves a hand desperately.

'What did you say?' her companion demands.

'Those young men got inside,' Betty starts to explain. 'You know, those awful, those...'

'Yes, yes, I know. Awful. Hooligans. That's what happens when you let the working class go on holiday.'

'Yes, quite,' says Betty with some reserve, remembering her own rather humble origins. 'The thing is, Harriet, the thing is the working class have just climbed into your hotel bedroom.'

'Good grief!' Harriet stands alarmed. 'Call the manager!'

From above them comes a challenge. 'Fuck off you bunch of dagokrauts!' And then the three on the balcony break into chanting. 'We're the best, we're the best, we're the best...' Below them the small crowd looks up in awe as three bottles of retsina are raised simultaneously, momentarily interrupting the mindless but alarming battle cry that haunts football stadiums and railway stations across Europe. 'They are truly mad,' one of the Norwegians sings out in disbelief. They explain to Alexos that they had seen them go up the hotel ladder, had tried to stop them, and encountered only abuse and threat of physical harm.

'English,' a lone voice says. 'Crazy people. Crazy.'

Harriet Simmons, now well out of the bar and on the beach catches the comment and responds. 'What was that? I demand to know who said that!'

'We're the best, we're the best, we're the best...' the chorus continues up in the air. 'We're the best, we're the best, we're the best...'

'Who said we were crazy? I demand to know!' Strident, slightly apart from the crowd, she faces them. 'How dare you say we're crazy! We are not!'

'Fuck you all. Fuck all you fuckers!'

'Harriet, come back at once!' Betty pleads, sensing chaos.

'Shut up, woman!'

'Oh!' Betty catches her breath.

'I demand to see the manager!' Harriet Simmons declares.

'Yes, madam,' Alexos responds courteously.

'Get those boys down from that balcony. Good heavens, one of them might fall and hurt himself.'

'Yes, madam. You have a point.' But the logic

throws Alexos and the crowd into total paralysis and they watch, frozen, as one of the young men collapses over the balcony railings and falls, screaming, onto the tarpaulin that covers the bar. Alexos whispers a brief prayer to God. The crowd gasps and stands back. 'There, I told you,' Harriet Simmons says triumphantly. 'Didn't I?' She watches, eyes wide, as the young man rolls across the tarpaulin and falls with an awful thud onto the beach.

'My God, he's dead,' someone says.

'Of course he's not dead,' Harriet pronounces, 'but he is drunk. Fetch an ambulance.'

THURSDAY

Things happen in Tiryns. I feel it necessary to say this because if there were a single generalisation about my life at home in Silbury it would be that nothing happens. I could not say, for example, that things really happen with George. They come and go without real impression. Of course, there are the children, but even they have assumed their own predictable rhythms. But here, things seems to happen. What is it about people on holiday? It's as if they find themselves suddenly free to do the first damn thing that comes into their heads. Today a young car dealer from Tonbridge went out into the Bay of Argos on a pedallo with his girlfriend. They had with them her daughter from a marriage just over. The wind came up, and they found themselves five kilometres out from the beach, unable to return. Why are people so stupid? I asked George the same question, which was hardly a smart thing to do, and he said nothing. 'Say something, George,' I told him. It was evening and we were eating lamb at Vangelis' on the beach.

'So,' he said in his usual flippant way, 'the wind came up, and they got unlucky.'

The man is meant to be a headmaster, but he lacks any moral control of his life. He uses words in a vacuum. But again, I wonder, is it just George, or something more than that?

Today, one of the three young Englishmen nearly killed himself. George said he would have done if he hadn't already been totally paralysed by drink. Falling from the third floor of The Delphi would have been the end of most people, but all he got was a broken arm. I can't find it in myself to feel great concern, but know that I should. Ann Preston continues to fascinate me. I watched her today, standing next to a Greek I haven't seen before. It was on the beach and they were talking - but what about? She is a very handsome woman, very intense. Now, the night is pitch black, almost quiet, and I am thinking in a way I am not used to. I hear questions which are my own but I don't know the answers. I wish I could think nothing, feel nothing, just lie here, like the two girls.

There are two girls, about eighteen, who just lie on the beach, day after day, and read. They read endlessly, and say nothing. One is blonde, with long hair, long legs, but her friend is darker. Now, even with my eyes shut I can't remember more of their faces, or bodies. They just lie there and read, on their backs, then on their fronts. Every now and again one of them gets up and wades out into the water, just to the waist, splashes about a bit, and then returns. And then it is the turn of her friend. And so it goes on.

Julia does not write any more than this on this Thursday evening. The night closes down on the small town, and a tumult of voices imposes silence. Cicadas. Wind. Sea. There are other intrusions, fractions of exchanges, the sound of glasses moving, ouzo, and echoing above on the balcony where Ann Preston sits alone another glass moves, and a cigarette is lit, and another observer watches the stars.

Inside, George is asleep. Tom has been asleep for hours, but Gail is restless, and her mother catches her murmurs. Julia stares at Aphrodite through a wall of blackness, pure black, lit behind by the lights on the far shoreline, and she wonders if she'll have the courage one night to whisper up in the dark to the woman sitting up there on the balcony above her; or if, like so much in her life, she will do nothing.

FIVE

At the age of eleven Tom is already in possession of a highly developed sense of curiosity, tinged with a certain cynicism rarely found in someone of his years. The cynicism is obvious to those adults in his close company, and is a trait often put down to having to live with his father. To his father it is put down to an unusual level of maturity, and also a probable result of having to live with his mother and put up with other adults.

On the Friday George's camera disappears again, though George does not doubt for a moment where it is.

It is ten thirty in the morning. It is very still, the sea is calm and the heat lies heavily on the bay. The geraniums and ivy at the front of The Villa Diana are dry and filmed with dust. Behind the bare breeze-blocks that now cover the hole at the base of the villa Georgios' cat decomposes quickly. Julia lies reading under their umbrella, just one recognisable body on a beach full of people, some prone, some restless, a constantly moving mix of colour and shape. George stands on the steps of the villa, binoculars in one hand, a bottle of Amstel beer in the other. He sees Jo Bullock standing in the sea, moustache bristling under a white floppy hat, unashamedly watching two young women wade past him, breasts high and bare. On the beach Mary Bullock watches her husband. Her children lie still, reading. Mo Greenbaum stands arms folded on his chest near Georgios' ice cream cart, and catches George's eye as he stands on the villa steps. They wave at each other. George scans the sea with his binoculars, examining pedallos and surfboards.

Across the bay Stavros lifts his hand from Gail's breast and catches light flashing from the direction of the beach. He spits over the balcony with contempt. Probably some pervert with binoculars. Gail is sleeping, in spite of his attention. He tells himself that this girl will kill him if he doesn't watch out. He must be getting old. Then, without warning, he thinks of Gail's mother. Family Moore. Julia Moore. His skin tenses. He knows it's his sixth sense, telling him something, and as if in recognition of the approaching possibility of unfaithfulness the soft imagined lushness of Julia Moore's mouth presses down on his arms, and wrists, and moves under Gail's blind eyes to the lower regions of his stomach.

Back on the beach George tells himself that Tom, that little bugger, has got the bloody camera.

Six hundred metres away Tom Moore pushes

mercilessly on the pedals of a pedallo, his small brown body alive with energy, young muscles giving and swelling, tendons playing along his legs. His eyes tell of secrets, deep knowledge, and his young inner eye flashes scenes of bare breasts, long legs, uncovered thighs, unmatchable forests of bodily hair carved in delightful forms between soft, brown, glistening limbs.

Tom has discovered a small colony of nudists, devout, holistic followers of mother nature, based in Graz, Austria, for most of the year but now oiled up, naked and hidden from the outside world on the far side of Aphrodite. His relentless curiosity had led him in the early hours of the morning out to Aphrodite on a pedallo, and there at half past eight, while his parents and most of the visitors to Tiryns still slept, he had watched from behind a boulder as three men and three women passed by, naked in a power boat. One of the women had been standing, her hair swept back by the wind, her breasts magnificently high, and it was then that Tom had felt his blood pulse and surge in a wave of madness that threatened to overtake him and command the pedallo to tear after the power boat.

He returned to the villa as fast as possible, determined to secure his father's camera and binoculars.

Now, he is back with the camera. The

binoculars, in the drawer by his father's bed, had been too risky. Tom's pedallo edges round the western point of Aphrodite, the island's left breast mounting ruggedly into the sky, grey-cragged and forbidding at such close distance. He searches the shoreline ahead of him, eyes moving swiftly, at first with disappointment, but finally with a whispered 'gotcha' he spies them. He secures the pedallo in a small inlet, hauling it up onto the rocks. His small body sweats. He climbs across grey rocks, stocky heather, brown dry grass; he leaps like Pan, landing with firm feet, and grinning as he does so. Two hundred metres away George pedals hard in pursuit. Through his binoculars he sees his son scrambling like a young goat among the lower sweep of Aphrodite's left breast. He nods to himself, sees the camera slung over his son's shoulder, and is reassured. How in God's name did he get such a son? The first urgings of puberty drive Tom round the rocks and onto a safe ledge, where he squats and looks down at the Austrians, who have provided themselves with a decent sized raft, against which they have moored their boat. Holism is not of much interest to Tom but he does know a naked human body when he sees one and right now he is particularly interested in naked female bodies. As indeed is his father.

From their separate positions, only twenty

metres apart, father and son look down in astonishment at the six naked Austrians standing on their heads. Tom aims the camera. His father focuses the binoculars.

Silence bears down on Aphrodite and its small group of players, the watchers and the watched. A lone bird freezes across the upper limits of the frame. The six bodies subside. Music breaks out. The Bee Gees. Tom wrinkles his nose and his father remembers dark nights in the seventies. Below them the Austrians show that they are well versed as they move in unison through a series of rehearsed steps, this time the right way up. Tom's camera does not stop. George feels his way towards the boy, and hisses. His son blanches. 'Christ, Dad! Do you have to?'

'That's my camera, you little bugger.'

Tom proffers it at once, and George relents. 'What stop?' he asks.

The boy does not understand.

'F what?' George insists.

'What F?'

'What F stop?' George demands. The whispering continues behind the boulder. Below them the Austrians continue with the Bee Gees unwittingly supervising a session of bastardised Canadian Airforce exercises.

'On the camera, Tom. Was it F11?'

Tom shrugs his shoulders and declares that his father is weird. George examines the camera, adjusts the stops, gives his son the binoculars, and aims the camera at the group.

'You scared the shit out of me,' Tom confesses to his father.

'You should've asked about the camera,' George tells him.

'You were asleep.'

'You should've woken me.'

'Mum would've gone apeshit.'

George does not deny the observation.

'What are they doing, those guys?' Tom points down at the Austrians. 'Is that foreplay?'

'God knows,' his father answers. 'They probably believe in something.'

Tom considers the explanation and concludes, as often seems to be the case, that his father hides things from him. 'Something to do with the end of Christianity, something like that,' George continues. Tom eyes his father warily. Adrenalin pumps round his small body. Down below the Austrians are standing, man to woman, embraced. 'That's foreplay,' George says. 'Yuk,' Tom replies. The observation is made behind raised binoculars, and accompanied by the click of the camera, which quite unexpectedly in this silence echoes away up towards the summit.

The Austrians look up, alarmed. 'Oh, shit!' Tom yells. 'Let's get the hell out of here!'

'You two are very silent about where you've been,' Julia says, intrigued, probing. George and Tom Moore read books, listen and commune silently, agreeing not to reply. 'I watched you pedal out to the island,' she continues, prodding her husband with her left foot. They are on the beach, around the umbrella. The sun is fierce.

'And then I watched you pedal back.'

'OK, OK,' Tom says.

'So?'

'So nothing.'

'No, Tom. There always has to be a so something.'

George regrets his son's lack of years, and listens as Julia drags on with the inevitable. 'So, what did you go to see? And why two pedallos?' George nods. The logic, as usual, is bloody relentless. 'For one thousand drachmas less you could have taken one pedallo. You'd be less tired. You could have been together, father and son. What in the bloody hell has been going on?'

'We got chased by some Austrians,' Tom says. 'Big ones.'

'Oh?' Julia replies, genuinely impressed.

'Yeh.'

'Shut up,' his father advises.

'I'm interested,' Julia continues, propping herself up on her elbows. 'So?'

'But we made it OK,' Tom concludes.

'Tell me more,' she insists.

'That's it,' George says.

'The guys came after us, the men and the women, but we had clothes on and they didn't and when they realised that they stopped. If you're going to make war you've got to get dressed first. Even they tumbled to that.'

Julia looks in horror at her son. 'And where,' she adds on an even stronger note, 'is your sister?'

'With that guy, I guess. Or another. She's an animal.'

'I wasn't talking to you, Tom. I was talking to your father.' Who lies on his front, looking down the beach to where Maeve approaches, long brown body, black bikini bottom, breasts full, brown, bare, the whole package purposeful, intense.

'Hi,' she lets the word fall like ice cream, and George feels it slip across his chest. She stops, and Julia has to look up. She feels naked but is not, wearing as she is a large yellow T-shirt. It is Maeve who is naked, standing over her husband, confident, pushing herself on them. Julia hates her. 'Hi, Maeve.' Julia's voice is a butterfly, and as it flutters it leaves her breathless.

Tom examines the adults. His eyes squint. He has never seen so much female flesh in his life.

'Martin said,' Maeve says to George, and then smiles at Julia, 'why don't we, you and Julia, have dinner together?' Not a question, Julia reflects, and addressed to George, she has to remember, and almost certainly nothing to do with Martin at all. Lying bitch. 'Yes, please, wonderful,' Julia answers. 'Actually, I was going to suggest...' They smile at each other. Julia is sure that Maeve will have George, and knows that George will not stop her, but if only she knew what she knows she wouldn't even bother. Why are men so weak? George smiles at his wife and knows what she is thinking and tells himself he was never on the market as a bloody sexual athlete, anyway, for Christ's sake. 'So, what have you been up to?' Maeve's question is lightning, discharging, freeing the air. Tom looks up at Maeve, and dares his eyes to wander round the blackness of the bikini bottom and into the roundness clutched between her legs, and his father catches him doing it, and he too thinks of Maeve, and Julia sees them both, and feels the sea creeping up towards them and tells herself she intends to lie down in this place in the next few days with a real man who is going to make her scream.

George wonders what it is that can make an evening so pleasant when the main preoccupation, namely eating, is such an appalling experience. The four of them approach this aspect of the evening with a certain deliberation.

'How's your lamb?' George asks Martin.

'It's pork. It's OK.'

'Looks like lamb,' George says, eyeing the plate.

'Souvlaki,' Martin insists. 'Pork souvlaki. Want some?'

'Pork, lamb, what's the difference?' Maeve says. 'I mean, cooked like this?'

Julia stares at her own food and says, 'I don't think I've had a decent meal since we came. Maybe I could be a vegetarian,' she adds thoughtfully. 'Probably will. I mean, how badly can you cook a bean?'

'You've always liked meat,' George reminds her. Maeve is wearing long earrings, streams of thin silver that fall on each side of her face like waterfalls. George is opposite her and his foot touches hers. He thinks of his fingers floating in those silver waterfalls, reaching for her ears, her hair. Then he turns to Martin, and smiles. These two are his friends. He loves this self-styled European, his neat round face, his quiet blue eyes, the woman he lives with. They are sitting round a table on the beach, one of ten tables set in front of

The Ship. Coronisi is lit up. Across the bay the lights of Plaka beach are a line of single lamps. Dimitris, the owner, has assured them that it will be a perfect evening.

'It will be a perfect evening,' he had said, ushering in the moon, and stars, and night itself.

'How can you fail with such a host?' Maeve had observed. 'Such orchestration.'

Maeve's eyes are dark and very deep, and when George looks at her they are part of the night itself; he tells himself that this could be the end for the Headmaster of St Mary's.

Cats stalk the tables, and at times leap on the rush-seated chairs. A table of young women eye Dimitris, and George watches them. He wonders what it is in that man which makes these young girls from England openly invite him to use them as he wishes. He is a small man, compact, with an open face. What in God's name makes his conquests so possible? George turns his attention to the girls. One is tall, much taller than can be comfortable. She leads the others, talking loudly. Another has light brown hair and is deeply tanned; her eyes are pale blue. She watches the owner of The Ship, signalling to him what he has known since she first sat down, that she is here, waiting.

A kitten sits on her lap. She touches it, and the animal closes its eyes. Dimitris observes quietly, and smiles, praising the cat for playing its part.

Julia half knows what is happening and is genuinely shocked. 'Good god, the girl is brazen.'

'What about the man?' Maeve says quietly.

Martin looks out towards Coronisi and the small incoming waves. Julia imagines Dimitris and the girl, walking naked in the shallows by the beach. George studies the shadows on Maeve's face, and sees himself astride her, riding like the Devil on a black horse.

They order coffee and metaxa. The table of young women is now empty, except for the one with light brown hair and blue eyes. Dimitris sits next to her. George grins knowingly at Martin. Julia, however, suddenly feels ill. It starts as a gnawing in the lower pit of her stomach, then moves upwards, growing in urgency. She pales, and trying to identify causes, examines her plate.

'You OK?' George asks.

'Yes. No.'

She gets up, and is unsteady. It is Martin who reaches out for her and catches her hand. 'I'll walk you back,' he says. The Villa Diana is only fifty metres away. Maeve and George watch as Julia and her escort move slowly across the beach towards the steps. 'Maeve.' George's voice is a light whisper. She leans towards him and her mouth brushes his. They get up. Dimitris watches them and in spite of the current instant diversion with the young woman beside him registers that these four have not yet paid their bill. He will tell them tomorrow. Who? The small round one, or the headmaster?

Outside the Villa Diana there is a tree which climbs to the balcony where Ann Preston sits with her cigarette. Maeve and George lean against the tree and they kiss. 'Christ,' he says. 'You're a very immoral headmaster,' she tells him. 'You smell, I don't know, strangely,' he whispers. Maeve considers the comment, and bites his lip. George stares at the dark face of the breeze blocks behind the tree and realises he has been mistaken. It is not Maeve who smells strangely. It is the cat.

Above them they hear a voice, quiet, understanding, and then Julia, being very ill. 'Oh, God, Martin,' they hear her voice ringing out. 'I'm so sorry. I'm so sorry.'

'Keep your head down,' Martin tells her authoritatively.

'Oh, God!'

Maeve and George listen under the tree. Her fingers move across his back; he is roused and presses against her. Julia retches again. 'Martin is a saint,' Maeve says. 'I'm not,' George admits, moving his hand against the inside of Maeve's thigh. Huskily, she asks, 'What is that smell?'

'A cat,' he says. 'It's dead.'

The chain is pulled and seconds later the entire villa erupts as Julia yells, Martin shouts out 'Holy shit!' and the youngest Preston boy almost falls over the balcony in his eagerness to find out what is going on. All three Prestons look down and see Maeve and George motionless, bodies pressed together. Inside the villa Martin stands in awe in the corner of Julia's bedroom, while she stands against the door of the lavatory. The lavatory bowl itself seethes; water and old sodden pieces of paper well up over the sides and slop onto the floor in a continuous surging act of regurgitation. Martin stares in disbelief at the mess that washes around his feet. 'I'm so sorry,' Julia repeats, desperately. 'I didn't mean to do,' and she gesticulates at the floor, 'all this.'

Maeve and George breathe the same breath. 'What all this?' George whispers, and then falls silent as Tom contributes to the observations. 'Oh, shit Mum, you sure cocked up in a big way this time.'

'Shut up, damn you, you horrible little bugger!' George hears his wife shout back.

'And what's he doing here?' Tom's voice floats out of the window, undoubtedly referring to

Martin. George's hands drop away from Maeve's body and his body subsides. Lust is over. 'Not tonight,' he verbalises.

'Well,' she agrees, 'not after all that, I suppose. Pity.' They stand apart.

George contemplates the wall. 'That,' he says, 'was a mistake.'

'What 'that'?'

'The wall.'

'What wall?'

George retreats; too much to explain, too late at night. Martin reappears from the villa. 'She OK?' George enquires.

'Bit of a mess in your bathroom,' Martin tells him.

'Ah.'

'Greek plumbing.'

'That's what we thought.'

'She's OK. Julia.' Martin drops her name and scratches his neck. Maeve has been playing about again. Bitch. 'Looked a bit white, my friend. Like fish. You know, fishy sort of stuff. Came slopping out all over the bloody place.' His feet kick at the sand. 'Might have been some of the lamb, come to think of it. Why can't these buggers cook?'

George is overwhelmed by the emotion, and

asks 'Where is she?'

'Passed out on the bed.'

'Really?' George is intrigued.

'The boy's with her. Where did he get that funny accent?'

'MTV. Did you see Gail? My daughter.'

'Oh, yes. Her. No.' And they all stare out at Coronisi, alight, a strong image of rock and strength in this fragile part of the night. Which is again interrupted by the chorus. 'Hell, not again,' Martin says.

'Not again,' Mo Greenbaum echoes, unseen not fifty metres away on the upturned hull of a fishing vessel.

Ann Preston draws on her cigarette. Maeve's body tenses. 'We're the best, we're the best, we're the best, we're the best, we're the best.'

'Dear God, not again,' another voice rises from the beach. 'Please.' George recognises that it belongs to Jo Bullock. 'Amen,' Martin says. 'I don't know,' Maeve says thoughtfully. 'I quite like them.'

Some thousands of years before this morning men came to the promontory of rock that guards the northern edge of the bayhead where the modern town of Tiryns stretches along the beach.

They climbed the rocks and stared out to sea, and saw how well this place commands the head of the Bay of Argos. And long before the Turks and the Cretans and the other traders built the town of Tiryns they created the town and fortress of Assini.

The hull of Kostas' boat moves just perceptibly in the first real light of early morning, close to the bulky rock promontory of ancient Assini. Kostas is one of half a dozen already out in this early morning, though on this particular occasion his fishing gear is still stowed. He sees today as a holiday, his birthday in fact, in part devoted to the young English boy who now swims unseen beneath the hull of his boat. Kostas smokes, looks up at young Stavros' villa higher up the cliffs along the bay, and recollects that it is the young boy's sister who has taken so much of Stavros' attention over the past week.

Tom is a seal, and imagines his nostrils closing tight, and the short close fur protecting him from the water. He reaches out with his hands and propels himself upwards with the flippers. The water breaks and a mask and snorkel move up close to the edge of the boat. Kostas looks over, looming, and is like a giant to the eyes behind the mask. 'You OK?' the Greek shouts down, and

Tom waves back at the large fat man in the tight brown T-shirt. 'Good,' and Kostas lights another cigarette. Eight o'clock. Another hour, maybe, and he'll take the boy home. He remembers he has promised the Moores dinner that evening. Another hour. Maybe a little more. Beneath the water again Tom pursues legends of his own making. Dead men's voices are holed up in the endless arrays of crevices and ledges just centimetres below the surface. But the dead are guarded. Sea anemones, mauve and cream, sifting sand and water as the sea surges, and armies of sea urchins, black, armed, guarding secret lairs. Tom sails close to them, excited by the danger. Old shells lie half buried in the sand. He passes a sea-hare, quite perfect, tantalisingly blue and grey. Rounder, patterned cones lie mostly broken by the movement of water, the dead reminders of the black spined living creatures that cling to the rocks. Then a light. Glittering. He swims back, and down, further than he anticipates, reaches out a hand, but misses. Kostas leans over the boat, and watches the boy dive again. The seal moves down. Tom's legs are together, and his body thrusts down. He seizes another touch of light, then comes to surface warily, unsure of what he has in his hand. Slowly he swims in towards the rocks and hauls himself out of the water. It is a coin. He lifts his face quickly, and scans his immediate and then more distant horizons. Kostas and his boat are only a few metres away. Tiryns itself is faceless, and he feels safe. He culls his small store of history and tells himself that he has almost certainly found something very old, and that very likely there are many more such coins, hidden in those rocks below the water. He dives again, and again, forcing the air into his young lungs, gasping, then a seal once more, seeking the prey beneath the rocks. He pulls up five coins, but his fingers tell him there are a lot more. The coins disappear into the pocket of his swimming trunks, and he is silent on his way back in the boat.

Kostas grins. 'Like it?' he asks.

Tom nods. He might be famous. He might get hundreds of pounds. Of course, he'll have to tell his father, but he doesn't want the others to know. And definitely not the Greeks.

He schemes.

Tomorrow he'll come back out in a pedallo and dive again, maybe with his father.

'Good boy,' Kostas says, still grinning. 'Swim like a fish.' He wonders how many coins the boy has found. Smart little English boy. But then that is an essential part of the game. Why play with fools when God provides the occasional angel?

So it is. The boy will go back and tell his father,

the headmaster. Kostas thanks God in a brief aside that none of his children go to school under such a man. Yes, the boy will talk, and his father will come, and he, Kostas, will be there first to make sure the supply of coins is replenished. And of course, to help them, to pledge them to secrecy as it really is a small act of pillage and plunder, if they look at it from the point of view of the Greek government. His charge for all this advice and assistance is merely nominal. Three thousand drachmas a coin, a sum which is usually willingly handed over. After all, not everyone has such coins from ancient Mycenae and Argos. The money is also necessary as a capital investment, Kostas reflects, as he has to pay his brother, Vassilis, five hundred drachmas each to make the damn things.

Tom smiles warmly as they run into a fresh breeze that comes in round from Nafplion, sweeps round the harbour, and meets the small boat head on. Kostas breaks into song, and claps his hands. He thinks with joy of the tens and tens, and maybe hundreds, of secret, hoarding, happy Britons, the housewives in London and the bankers in Liverpool, all of them knowingly guilty of taking ancient coins out of Greece without a licence, but unknowingly victims of a quiet act of retribution which he, Kostas, has been carrying out at

Andreas' instigation for many years now. It is not an inconsiderable act of retaliation, really, by a couple of individuals on a nation which had plundered the marbles from The Parthenon and stored them away in that museum in London. Kostas sees Tom smiling, and Kostas grins, and much to Tom's surprise says 'Kostas one, Elgin nil.'

Tom disagrees with his father's point of view and argues with him volubly on the beach. 'Why not?' he demands.

'Because it's part of their heritage,' George tries to explain.

'What's that?'

'National treasure. Like the Crown Jewels, for example.' A few metres away Jo Bullock catches the conversation, and listens.

'The Crown Jewels aren't at the bottom of the sea,' Tom says fiercely.

'That's not the point. The coins belong to Greece. They belong to the Greeks.' George surprises himself with this act of reason, but nonetheless is sure that he is right.

'The Greeks don't know about them,' Tom points out

'Just because you don't know something is there doesn't mean that it isn't,' George tells him with authority.

Tom considers this and then says, 'I want them. They're mine.'

'No. I'm sorry.'

'I'm going to keep them, anyway.'

George relents. 'OK, but no more. Did Kostas see you?' Tom shakes his head, and remembers the fat man smiling at him. A second of doubt fuses into shadows of thought in Tom's mind; but he is too young.

'Oh, shit everything,' he says, concluding the interview with his father.

Jo Bullock watches the child get up and go, and having thought a while decides to have a quiet word with Kostas. It would be nice to take home a few old coins.

Martin Rushton has observed Andreas, marking him out on the first day as someone seemingly rather different from most of the shopkeepers and hotel owners in Tiryns, and yet someone he likes to think of as being rather typical - a Greek from whom he might learn something about Greece. He sees Andreas, a large man who keeps his strength and the tautness of brown skin over muscle hidden behind expensive clothes from Milan. He sees someone reserved in other ways, who speaks quietly, without the strong declamatory tone of his friends and associates; yet Martin Rushton has learnt nothing about Minoa Travel nor about Andreas' time in London. However, Andreas has found out about the Englishman, and retreated. He resents the notion of being collected, stored away, and referred to later in some expensive seminar; but he is amused by the Englishman's conceit about being European.

They are sitting on the beach at a long table outside The Ship. Andreas and Kostas sit at either end, Maeve and Martin are on either side of Andreas; then the Moores, and Jo Bullock with his wife, Mary, still very quiet. And Vassilis, like a great fat frog, wearing a huge straw hat with a blue ribbon round the brim. Vassilis, the maker of coins, the avenger of Elgin's rape and pillage of the marbles from The Parthenon. Kostas looks fondly round the table, until his eyes rest on the Mosses, the young couple he had found on the beach drinking cocktails at three in the morning. 'Cocktails?' he had queried, standing over them. 'Christ Almighty bloody hell.' The girl had nodded, young, too young to be married, he had told himself, long black trailing hair he had wanted to play with. Her husband was slumped in the chair next to her.

'Drunk?' Kostas had asked.

James Moss had grunted.

'Then go to bed, then ,' Kostas had suggested.

James had tried to deal with the suggestion, stood up, finished the cocktail sitting on the table in front of him, then passed out, toppling over his chair, leaving his legs in the air and his head resting on the sand.

'Too many Bombays,' Elaine, his wife, had explained.

'What?' said Kostas, confused.

'Bombers,' muttered a strangled voice from the sand. 'One measure rum, one measure..' but his voice had died away in the effort. Kostas had looked in alarm at Elaine, who had shrugged her shoulders and said, 'Don't ask me the measures, Kostas. I never drink them. Not Bombays. I mean, look what they did to him.'

Kostas reflects on the memory, then turns his attention to the present. So, now it is time to eat and drink. Dimitris' wife is a good cook. Andreas will talk about this and that and the English will be impressed. Later, the English will get drunk and go to bed and his own friends will come and they will end the evening playing cards and backgammon. Dimitris stands small and dark in the shadows. He has known Andreas for thirty seven years; as children they had swum in the bay. Tiryns had been no more than a strip of cottages, their owners farmers of oranges. Today the farmers are older and richer. The European Union has poured money into the town and the tourists have spent millions. Dimitris' father was a poor man, but now his son rides a 750 CC Honda and sleeps with the daughters of Germans from Hamburg. Kostas beams down on the assembled table. Dimitris' wife brings on fish, lemon chicken with roast potatoes, deep fried courgettes, salads with feta cheese and green pepper rings, olives and cucumbers, tzatziki and fresh bread. They drink from litre carafes, dry retsina and white demestica. George Moore views the food, and recognises quality he hasn't experienced so far; Julia prays that he will lay off the demestica. James Moss wonders how many Blue Lagoons and Sledgehammers he and his wife had consumed before coming to The Ship. 'Three each,' he whispers to her. She holds up four fingers. 'You OK?' he asks with obvious tenderness, and she nods back. At home he has just bought a new black Golf. Elaine has just bought into a local hairdressing shop in Chingford. He has had his eye on a recently converted cottage further out in Essex. At twenty four he is on the way up.

They both smile at Kostas. 'Happy birthday, Kostas.' They raise their glasses. Elaine looks round the table discreetly, drinks, stores in images of faces, the table, the sea beyond, Coronisi alight with floodlamps, the noise of the town to the left and right, images that she hopes will return with her to England, reserved for friends, and quiet conversations about what was done and where.

It has become known on the beach that Martin is a film maker. That he is a maker of video films is not recognised, and that he is a name in the field of inter-cultural training is not known at all. So it is that there is a considerable amount of nudging and posturing, lighting of cigarettes and unnatural fidgeting when he enters The Ship during the daytime, or when he is passed by on the street. Martin himself does little to clarify the situation. He allows it to happen. Maeve watches and wonders if he doesn't let things go too far sometimes. Night deepens. Bottles of demestica come and go. Cats gather round the table, walking, rushing, waiting for hands to reach down, the occasional scrap to fall, a chair and plate to be unwisely unattended for just a second or two. Andreas is deep in thought and has been for some time. 'You,' he says suddenly to Martin Rushton, and his voice is aggressive, 'know something about the English.' Martin hesitates, recognising it as an unusual approach. 'I am English,' he says by way of explanation. 'And I am Greek,' Andreas replies, sitting back in his chair and smiling. Martin isn't so sure where this will lead. 'You make films to tell people this and that,' Andreas continues. 'To instruct. To train. So, you know something.' Maeve watches her husband closely, and her face moves into a smile as she senses what the Greek is up to. 'Well, that's right,' Martin acknowledges. 'About this and that, yes.'

'Ah,' Andreas says triumphantly. 'About.' The word hangs heavy and victorious.

Jo Bullock catches the conversation at the other end of the table and announces to no one in particular, 'His English is pretty good. Wonder where he learnt it?'

'So, tell me why the English are so violent,' Andreas continues, his voice falling, a concluding question which is also a statement.

'Who says we are?' Jo Bullock demands, thrusting forward across the table. Vassilis sits next to Mary Bullock and starts talking to her, something which no one notices except for Kostas. 'It's only isolated groups,' George says, wishing that Jo wouldn't make such a fool of himself. 'Hooligans. The Millwall crowd.' 'Oh, George, our hooligans aren't isolated,' Julia reproaches. 'Those football fans.'

'Not a logical collocation, really,' Maeve says

quietly, 'I mean, when you think about it. Football fans like football, supposedly. These people are thugs. They like thuggery.' 'Ah,' Andreas says, and looks hard at the woman he has not so far studied. George catches the glance and is jealous. 'The point is,' Andreas continues, 'they are only an example. What about your armies? The English soldier has a reputation for violence.'

'Armies are meant to be violent,' Martin says in a rush. 'You Greeks had a go at the Persians. And the Turks. And each other, come to that.'

'I mean,' Andreas says slowly, 'that individually you are violent people.'

George drinks demestica and thinks that he does not feel particularly violent. Jo Bullock does feel a pull, however, and announces, 'We're the best soldiers in the world, probably. Except for the Gurkhas.'

Vassilis' hand slips across Mary Bullock's thigh.

James Moss admits to his wife he'd also had a Zombie with a guy from Loughton when she'd been in the loo. She nods approvingly. 'Good?'

'Amazing,' her husband tells her. He grins, then notices Mary Bullock whispering to the Greek in the straw hat next to her. 'I don't think we are violent, as a race,' Martin says. 'Got to beware of stereotypes.'

A loud cry comes down to them from the edge

183

of the water, and three shadows run madly, incensed by a day's drinking. 'That lot,' says Jo Bullock. 'No, not them,' Andreas says deliberately. 'What do you mean?' Martin asks. 'He means that they are not what he is talking about,' Maeve says. 'But they're hooligans,' Jo Bullock says. Martin wishes he had more scotch with him. The local wine pounds at his temples and twists in his stomach. 'What does an inter-cultural expert know?' Andreas asks. Martin ignores the question. Jo Bullock realises for the first time that his wife is talking to the Greek next to her, a short but very well-built man with an eager face and an odd straw hat on his head. George and Julia Moore also realise that Mary Bullock is deep in conversation. The words that pass between the Englishwoman and the Greek, however, are muted, drowned in the surges of the sea. Jo Bullock is torn between what is happening on his left, and what is happening on his right. Julia Moore watches her husband watching Maeve. 'So,' Andreas says, 'you help people develop knowledge about themselves, and about others, other cultures.'

'More or less. Yes. Sort of.'

'And what if that person you are helping is a little bastard.'

'Well, that person might be,' Martin concedes. 'Often,' he adds quietly.

'I think,' Maeve whispers, and her voice is knowing, and the glint in her eye mischievous, 'that Andreas is talking about the difference between knowledge about and knowledge of. There are a lot of clever shits out there who know about things, but just watch them in action as human beings, just watch them. They're real little pricks. Am I right?' she finishes, turning to Andreas. Andreas stares back at her, and is happy that she has put his thoughts into words so directly.

'What's the difference?' Jo Bullock asks, confused. Vassilis and Mary Bullock slip away behind the tables and chairs and still raised umbrellas. They go unnoticed, except by Kostas, who is already well pleased with his birthday dinner. 'Do you like the Italians, the French, the Germans?' Andreas continues, his voice now raised. 'What about the Greeks? Do you like us? What do the English think of the Greeks?' Martin does not like the way this is going. It would never happen in England. 'What about national identity?' Andreas continues. 'It's a very real question for me, as a Greek. What do you feel about that?'

'You mean what about national and cultural identities within the European Union?' Maeve asks, and Julia hates her for asking the question, and wishes she had asked it first. George stares from one to the other, and then says lamely, 'actually, I'm on holiday. Bit serious, isn't it, all this?'

The cicadas sing, and Kostas lights a cigarette. Pity, he thinks. He'd hoped for more. But Jo Bullock is now agitated by his wife's absence, and more so by the absence of the Greek who had been sitting next to her.

'Should an Englishman aware of Greek culture act like a Greek in the presence of a Greek?' Andreas muses aloud. 'And the other way round, of course.'

'Oh, for Christ's sake!' Jo Bullock says, voice pitched high. They all watch him, waiting. 'I'm sorry,' he says, and gets up. 'Anybody see Mary go? You know, my wife.' The table answers in silence. The three shadows return and sit on the quay only metres away. They are silent now, but their presence is felt, and there is general uneasiness. Shades of the dead, Andreas thinks, squatting like a chorus of vultures at the edge of night. Jo Bullock storms down the beach, out of sight, and then back again, distraught. 'You OK?' James Moss ventures. Jo Bullock shakes his head. 'What has he got that I haven't got, damn him?' he cries out, confronting the sea.

There is silence, until one of the shadows on the quay raises his voice and shouts back, 'Your wife!'

'He was getting at me,' Martin says. They are lying side by side in bed. The hotel is quiet. Alexos had been in the lobby when they had come in and they had sat down with him to have a final scotch, and watch the small fishing vessels and some larger yachts ride up and down on their moorings. It was two o'clock in the morning before they went to bed, although further down the beach, away from the harbour and The Delphi, Tiryns is still very much alive, and the music from the discos will continue for another few hours.

'Of course he wasn't,' Maeve tells him. She lies quite still.

'Yes, he was. He was trying to make a fool of me.' Martin reaches out to his wife. 'Can we make love?'

'No.'

'Why not?'

'Because.' Maeve sinks into the darkness, dragging herself away from the room, away from her husband, till she strikes out, free, with the wind behind her and the open sky beyond. She feels herself move quickly upwards, and sees herself looking down on Tiryns, sees it as a shining yellow string of light in a crescent at the head of the bay, guarded by islands, which are dark dogs, crouching.

'I'd like to make love,' Martin tells her, and she curses him for bringing her back. She breathes in deeply and lies still, suddenly scared. A familiar dark shadow has come into the room and stands at the foot of the bed. She sees hands reaching down to her, hovering above her breasts. Fingers reach out and she feels them tearing into her, just below her shoulders. They are experts, these hands, and she lies rigid as they strip the flesh slowly, rolling it back piece by piece, stripping her breasts, her stomach, her thighs, until finally it is all folded at her feet so that she is left, a pulsating mess of blood and muscle. 'What are you thinking?' Martin demands. Put it back, she yells unheard, for God's sake put it back. Martin grunts at her silence, and down by the harbour a dog barks once.

FRIDAY

Today Tom found some old coins and got mad when George said he was wrong to have them. Why is it wrong for Tom to have the coins yet right for George to follow Maeve around like a rutting stag?

Tonight we had dinner with Kostas the fisherman and Andreas. I felt sorry for Martin Rushton; Andreas was obviously trying to needle him. I felt that both men, both Kostas and Andreas, were quietly laughing at us.

Something is about to happen here in Tiryns; I feel it in the air. Something terrible is about to happen. The cat gets worse; I'm not going to be able to stand it much longer. Tonight it's bad but about seven o'clock this evening before we went to The Ship the smell was terrible. Nobody sits in front of our villa any longer. There is a small exclusion zone several metres deep in front of the wall; the damn cat could ruin everything. We are now half way through our holiday, and tomorrow we go to Epidavrus to see Oedipus Tyrannus. It would seem that just about everyone is going: Harriet Simmons and Betty, the Prestons, the Greenbaums, that old couple, the Peters, whom I saw arguing violently in front of The Ship at lunchtime, he saying yes he had and she saying he was sure he hadn't, and a dozen fascinated Greeks standing by and watching the performance. It was Sarah Greenbaum who later explained what it was all about. Cancel the milk and the paper, she said. Had he or hadn't he? Only the Mosses aren't coming. For them the delights of Mai Tais and Margaritas far outweigh the dramatic concerns of Sophocles, and the bar of the Minotaur or The Ship is far more enticing than the old amphitheatre at Epidavrus.

Oh, Julia, Julia Moore. What in the name of God are you doing with your life, stuck like a well preened, well accepted rat in that awful little house? I wonder, when God thought of Hell, if he didn't think at times of 6, Darling Close. Of course, it's the money at the end of the day, the reason I go down the road and open that door and see that bastard sitting there. It's alright for Andreas to pontificate and state the obvious, or Martin to want people to change; it's all such a bloody game for them. But not for me. I go back there, and let that bloody man stand too close, and feel his breath, rank and glutted with all the smell of everything he carries in his stomach, and I know deep down that when I am not looking he carries me away at night to his bed.

And now George sleeps. Poor Jo Bullock,

worried about his wife with Vassilis, though for all I know all they do is talk. Why not? Maybe this is the only opportunity she's had in years.

SIX

On a clear morning in the ancient town of Mycenae a helmet was placed securely on its wearer's head. The helmet was shaped to the head and rose to a slightly pointed cone at the top, and covered the face as though with a three pronged fork, so that the eyes could see through the gaps between the tines. The helmet was heavy and strong, and made of bronze. As the soldier walked out into the courtyard the sun flashed across the side of his face, and then the back of his head.

The soldier was killed, and the helmet fell with him. Long afterwards it was found, and it exists today.

In the street called Apollon in the Plaka, just below the heights of the Acropolis, three young men from England stand in front of a shop. They have been in Greece for nearly a week and have come to Athens from Tiryns on a day trip. What attracts them in this particular shop are three cheap replicas of the helmet dug out of the ground at Mycenae. These replicas are true to the original in shape, but no more than that. They are constructed of riveted pieces of cheap brass, and shine with a dull yellow that will soon tarnish. Each of the helmets is topped by a long and thick crested plume, made of red and black nylon tufts. From time to time people take notice of the three young men. They stop and stare, and comment, and in fact there is a certain amount to comment on. As a uniform they wear blue shorts and T-shirts. These shirts bear messages relating to sexual intercourse. One of the young men is tall, the other two of medium build. One of the latter has an arm in plaster, the tall one has a black eye, all are burnt badly by the sun. Skin peels from their faces, backs and shoulders.

On the Saturday evening the group in Tiryns go to Epidavros. They stand and wait outside Minoa Travel, a tanned and well dressed group of tourists. The Bullocks are missing, which is noticed but not remarked on.

'Pee,' says Harriet Simmons forcibly. 'I can't think how you keep forgetting, Betty. E-PEE-davros.'

'Epi-DAV-ros,' Betty says in reply, pronouncing the name in exactly the same way she has always done and always will, with the stress firmly on the third syllable. Harriet Simmons snorts. 'I don't know, Betty, you're so, so uncultured. I mean, linguistically you're a peasant.'

Betty suffers the shame quietly for a second or

two, then says innocently, 'What is the capital of Greece, Harriet?'

'Why, Athens, Betty. Athens. You know that.'

'And what do the Greeks call the place?'

'Athenai,' Harriet says promptly. 'Why?'

'Exactly,' Betty says triumphantly.

'Exactly what? Good God, woman, you do infuriate me sometimes.'

Betty savours her victory, but as always is unacknowledged by the loser. Standing beside the two women Ann Preston holds an English translation of Oedipus Tyrannus in her hand and laughs quietly to herself at the exchange, but they are oblivious to her.

Maeve stands next to George Moore and whispers, 'Shall we have a drink later

He nods. 'I mean, the four of us,' she adds.

'Good idea. Should be back about twelve thirty. Could go to The Ship.'

Martin stands to one side, in spotless white trousers and a neatly ironed blue shirt. He's not sure about this outing. The play is in Greek and he's never had time for Greek tragedy. He'd rather sit down with a drink. 'Looking forward to it?' he asks Julia. 'Absolutely. Wouldn't miss it,' she tells him. 'Me, too, neither,' he says. 'I mean, it's not the sort of thing we normally do in Silbury,' she adds. 'What do you normally do?' he asks, spurred by sudden interest. 'Clean the house. Watch TV. Wait for George to get drunk.' The extended confession quietens them both. She reminds herself that she could have added that she also exercises her over-developed imagination and dreams of places far away from Silbury, and men far different from George.

A small cheer goes up from the assembled group as their bus manoeuvres its way down Tiryns' only and very busy street, sounding its horn and easing past parked cars with only a fraction of a centimetre to spare.

'Remind me of the story,' Martin says to George. 'I mean, the play.'

'Bloke lives with this woman, has a couple of kids, then the woman and bloke find out that though she's his wife she's also his mother, and the two kids are therefore also his sisters, woman kills herself, bloke sticks pins in his eyes. End of story.'

'Yuk,' Martin says, 'I remember now. Think I'd rather watch TV.' They board the bus and find that the back seats are already occupied. Three figures robed in black shrouds, faces hidden behind huge brass helmets with coloured plumes, each sit with a bottle of retsina firmly held in one hand. The nature of the confrontation between the three and each passenger as the bus is boarded is identical. It is enacted in total silence.

The bus moves off, and George feels an uneasiness around him, and a sudden sickness in his stomach. 'You've got to do something,' Julia whispers, and he knows that he should. 'I don't think they'll let them in. I mean, the guards at the gate.'

'It's awful,' Sarah Greenbaum agrees, further up the bus. 'I can't believe it. Do something, Mo, for God's sake.' 'What?' he asks reasonably. 'I don't know. something. You're a man, aren't you?'

'I think it's a crying shame,' Dina Peters says, rather more loudly and aggressively than the others. 'Oh, shut up,' her husband retorts, 'I'm not fighting any more of your battles. Not at my age.'

'Who let them on the bus?' Maeve asks no one in particular.

Tom kneels in his seat, facing backwards. 'They're weird,' he pronounces. 'Neat, but weird.'

'I think they're letting us down,' Gail says. 'For God's sake, Tom, don't ogle them.'

The bus passes the camp sites, passes old Assini, the orange groves, and climbs into more hilly territory. Tobacco leaves dry in fields to right and left. Many of the small whitewashed cottages on the side of the road bear signs which tell the traveller that fresh honey can be bought. The road twists and turns. The land is dry, a pattern of scrub and squat olive trees, tobacco and dry earth, and here and there a tall green cypress painted majestically up to the sky, now darkening as night begins to fall, and the stars appear. They reach Epidavrus with nearly an hour to spare before the start of the play. Their bus draws up in line with some of the others, which have driven to the amphitheatre from as far afield as Athens. Instinctively, the passengers on the bus get off quickly and disassociate themselves as completely as possible from the three robed figures, who stride off on their own at a tangent, driven by forces and intentions unfathomable to the others.

Ten thousand people march up the pathways to the amphitheatre, which still stands magnificent after centuries. The police and guards are efficient at marshalling these people in through the entrances and to their blocks. The theatre is lit by floodlamps, and the stage is bare except for a white wooden door. Two large scaffold structures stand at either side. There is an increasing hum of noise, as the hillside of scalloped tiered stone seating slowly fills. Languages mix, flashbulbs go off, and cigarette smoke rises up to the open sky. The bus load from Tiryns watch the gateways and the guards and police in hushed expectation, waiting for the confrontation which they are convinced has to take place. But the three young men do not appear and the group relies on rumour.

They were taken in the main car park is one theory Dina Peters projects. 'I mean, the Greeks aren't daft,' she explains. 'Taken away and locked up, that's my conclusion.' Betty is more of the opinion that they got to the gates, were stopped by the guards, and that there was then a fight. 'Don't be so barbaric, Betty,' Harriet had said impatiently. 'They probably took those helmets off and put them back on the coach. After we'd left.' Secretly, Harriet wishes she'd stayed in Tiryns. She's been to the amphitheatre before and sworn that she'd never repeat the experience. The seats are hard, she can't stand the cigarette smoke, the plays are interminable, and she can't understand a word. But here she is, back again, and she wishes she wasn't. 'It's a privilege to be here,' she says aloud. Martin looks in her direction, first at one woman, and then the other.

From elsewhere a voice sings out, 'What do you mean, it's not in English?'

'Shh! Roger. Shh!'

'Well, is it in English, or isn't it?'

'Of course it isn't,' comes the distressed reply. 'But you didn't tell me that,' the man says, defending himself. Martin tries to identify the pair but has to satisfy himself with the end of the encounter. 'Sophocles was a Greek,' the woman continues courageously. 'I know that!' her husband says waspishly. Only a second later his wife makes her defence, 'Well, so he wrote in Greek.'

The exchange is concluded. It is a dismissive, superior exit.

George relishes it and stores it away.

At nine o'clock the play begins. 'Oh, Christ,' comes the audible gasp from a purist, and the sentiment against the modern dress is expressed as a ripple of complaint in a dozen languages which moves up and down the terraces. Oedipus has a magnificent voice and a great presence, and George watches in awe as the language is thrown powerfully into the hills. He sits close to his wife. She feels him against her and at one stage in the performance reaches for his hand. Exits and entrances are dramatic, and the actors hurl themselves about the stage. George is enthralled by the use of the two scaffold towers, to look outwards to the hills and sea, or house the chorus, who clamber up the structures and declaim to the audience.

For all of them the unease created by the three young men recedes. They are forgotten, except by George, who senses foreboding as the play draws

to its close. It happens as the messenger speaks.
The crowd is riveted as she stands in the centre,
speaking of the mother wife hanging by the neck.
They listen and hear of Oedipus, ripping the
brooches from the wife mother's robes. They listen
on. All except for George, whose secret fear opens
his eyes and focuses them on three shadows
climbing one of the scaffold towers.

'Oh, God,' he says. 'No. Please, no.'

As the messenger tells of Oedipus thrusting the
brooch pins into his eyes three lone forms squat
silently on the top of the tower. Knowledge that
they are there ripples through the group from
Tiryns. Their attention is confused. The shared
perception of the contradiction in the combination
of ancient tragedy and the antics of a more modern
era creates a vibrant, growing tension,
unrecognised at first by anyone outside the group.

'I want to go,' Julia whispers.

'You can't,' George tells her.

'But what are they going to do?' she insists,
echoing a fear common to them all. In fact, the
three do nothing but sit, and in doing so impose
slowly but persistently an awareness of their
presence on groups here and there in the audience,
groups which then are agitated, and spread the

recognition. Slowly, like a coil unwinding, the audience reacts, noise murmuring, swelling, buzzing, so that the actors themselves hesitate, and are perplexed. But go on.

Accounts of the closing moments differ among the group. What is certain is that several guards and police go to the bottom of the tower, and it is equally certain that the three are not on the bus on the way home. It is also the case that the cast continue unabashed. Oedipus addresses the audience with bloodstained face, and the chorus delivers its final, fatal, lines. There is noise and shouting from the scaffold. George does not dare look in that direction but stares deep into the blackness of Maeve's hair as she sits taut and still in front of him.

The performance ends; the actors bow and are applauded. And then the audience leaves, most of them aware that something unscripted has happened, but far fewer knowing anything more than that. Betty hears that they were taken away in a police van. Dina disputes that, but says there was fighting down the hillside. Some say they were wearing helmets; others saw no sign of them. Some say they were chanting football songs; others maintain there was total silence. On the bus trip home there is a certain relief that there has been a climax, if an unclear one.

'I'd shoot them,' Terry Peters says.

Martin watches them all quietly. Privately, he thinks the incident has been one of the best of the holiday.

SATURDAY

Gail has been dumped by Stavros. I found her in the villa this morning, her face puffed up. She looked distinctly unhappy. 'It's your fault,' she yelled at me.

'What is?'

'If you hadn't made me go to that horrible play I'd still have him.'

'Who?' I'd asked, although I shouldn't have, really.

'Stavros.'

'What happened?'

'He met a girl at the disco, some cow from Scunthorpe. I knew it would happen. It's your fault.'

Naturally, I'm relieved and grateful, of course, to the cow from Scunthorpe. Still, I am sorry for her, as is George, who went out and bought her a large chocolate ice cream, which she ate, as though she hadn't eaten for weeks.

There was a council of war this morning, called by Jo Bullock, even though he was not at the play and was witness to nothing that happened. We sat, about a dozen of us, at the tables on the beach in front of The Ship. Jo was bright and cheerful, proudly displaying his wife. Everything must be OK with them now.

But how could it be?

Jo took command immediately. He sat at a table, with Mary demure at his side. Every now and again he drank beer from a bottle.

'Such a disgusting habit,' I heard Harriet Simmons say.

'The reason I called you,' he said, 'is that I thought we ought to take a stand. I know I wasn't there but I've been briefed by several of you about the incident and I think I've got a pretty clear picture.' I could see George bristle. 'I'd birch them,' Dina said. 'I would too. And their parents. I put it down to the sixties. John Lennon. That lot.'

'I think,' Jo said, 'we should make a stand. Agree on a policy so that the Greeks know we don't like it either.'

I could see that Maeve was immensely amused by all this. 'So, what do you propose?' she asked.

'I think we should write a letter of apology. Something like that.'

'And who are you going to send it to?' Martin queried. 'The entire population of Greece?'

'Well, it was just a thought. What about a letter

to the papers? What about a statement to the police?'

'Good God, man! Are you out of your mind?' Martin was genuinely alarmed, which poor old Jo couldn't understand. 'We've got to do something,' he said to Martin.

'We do have to do something,' Harriet Simmons echoed, and there was general agreement with that.

'I could try to make sure they're thrown out of wherever they're staying,' Jo said, brightening up. 'Anyone know where they're staying?'

James Moss lifted a sun hat that had slipped over his face and made his sole contribution. 'On the beach,' he said.

'Anyway,' Betty said, bringing things to a close, 'they're probably locked up.'

Which, reasonably, does seem to be the case.

Further evidence of George's moral decline came to light this evening.

Tiryns is awash with representations of sexual acts, of the human form about to have sex, or simply of the human form. All this is displayed on postcards, playing cards, and in shops professing to trade in what is called Greek Art. The evidence suggests that the ancient Greeks were technically

curious and probably quite supple.
Experimentation with various positions by the ancients is displayed on plates, curio boxes, brooches, and wall plaques. Amid this so-called art are racks of cards and calendars, cats, churches, scenes of sand and sea, and women; women from the back, from the front, lying down, standing up, leaning, bending, alone, in pairs, in multiples, with and without men.

Young girls and their mothers invite the tourist to come and browse, and buy. I found Tom in such a shop, having already made his purchase. Suspicious, I followed him back and asked to see what he had bought. 'Jeez, Mum, you're worse than a Nazi!' My suspicions began to firm. 'Show me!' I demanded.

'No!' He thrust a small brown bag into the drawer by his bed.

'Tom, you know I'm going to see it.'

His lips quivered. 'You won't like it, Mum, honest.'

'Then why did you buy it?'

'It's not for you, Mum.'

'OK, but if I won't like it, why did you buy it?'

'It's for Dad,' he said suddenly, his face brightening. Tom stepped aside and fell silent as I reached into the drawer and pulled out the playing cards. I looked through them. 'I told you,' he said.

'You don't like them. I told you.'

'It's called pornography, Tom,' I said quietly.

'I know,' he confessed. 'I bought them for Dad as a present. He seems a bit, you know, unhappy.'

'You bought these for your father?' He nodded. My son. How did this happen? 'As a present?' He nodded again. I took the cards away, gave Tom the two thousand drachmas he'd paid for them, and hid them in my suitcase. I then pledged the boy to silence and promised the matter was over. Later, I broached the matter with George and suggested he have a talk with his son. George promised, shook his head, and muttered something about corruption of the young. And then I went to lie down as George had promised to take me down to The Ship for a nightcap, and I wanted some rest before we went. I dozed off, and when I awoke the apartment was strangely quiet. Tom was asleep. Gail was out. On the balcony I could see my husband, absorbed over the pack of cards which he had liberated from my suitcase. I stood there, frozen, watching him examine them one by one under the light. I knew then, of course, what deep inside every woman really knows but tries her damndest to ignore. Men are corrupt, even the young. I stood, unseen, watching man and child. My husband, lusting after what he could not have; my son, who I was now quite sure had lied to me through his back teeth.

I tiptoed across to the boy's bed and went through his trouser pockets for the two thousand drachmas I'd given him.

SEVEN

Stavros has just spent the first part of the morning at Plaka beach, registering how things have changed over the last few years. The orange groves are now completely broken up by camp sites and small hotel complexes, many with swimming pools. But Plaka is not his territory. His, as he has explained to his cousin, Takis, stretches from the Hotel Delphi at one end of the beach to the promontory of Assini at the other. They pedallo back from Plaka, up to the last rocks of Assini, and then round and in towards Tiryns. The water is choppy and they pedal hard into the waves, slowing down every now and again as a speedboat approaches. Takis is several years younger than his cousin, and like many of his peers is in awe of Stavros' exploits, and party to the general rumour-mongering that builds gossip into myth, and legend into fact.

Takis is a virgin, a state of mind and body not unrelated to his difficulty with the English language. 'The tourist,' Stavros explains, 'usually lasts one or two weeks, but some last longer. Always treat the tourist with respect, even if they're smaller than you, and especially the boys. Boys grow and sometimes come back. They can be bigger than you, of course, and that can be dangerous. The English male tourist drinks a lot of beer and is difficult to talk to, but the English girl tourists are more interesting. They drink a lot of cocktails, which makes them laugh.'

'You make love with them,' Takis says. He stares down at an empty bottle of Loutraki water that floats by just a few metres from the pedallo. He reflects that the sea is getting dirtier, year by year.

'That is true,' Stavros concurs. 'But I ask them first.'

'What do you say?' Takis asks. 'I mean, when you ask them.'

'I tell them that they're beautiful.'

'Yes, but some of them aren't,' Takis points out.

Stavros ponders that and admits finally, 'Most of them aren't.' They slow down and drift. Two other pedallos come out from the beach on their way to Coronisi. 'What about Gail?' Takis asks. Stavros explains that the affair is over. 'But why?' Takis asks.

'Because on Friday she goes to Athens. Finish. It's better this way.' And on the Saturday morning there will be new planeloads on the beach, from Manchester, from Helsinki, from Gatwick and Stockholm. New eager, bemused faces. New, white, fresh bodies. New names. Hullo, you're a beautiful girl, I love you. And so it goes on through the summer, late nights and discos, beach and pedallo. Je t'aime, I love you, Ich liebe dich, you're a beautiful girl, I love your hair, your eyes, your perfume, yes your parents are fools, idiots, but you are wonderful and yes it was wonderful, of course I love you, but now I must say goodbye my darling. I'm sorry but I don't want to hurt you. On Friday you go to Gatwick, to Luton, and it will break my heart. No, I am not a bastard, I am just a poor Greek, goodbye.

'You must eat a lot of yoghurt and honey and vitamin C,' Stavros says in a rush, suddenly protective of his cousin's innocence.

'Why?'

'So you won't catch anything, idiot.'

'Catch what?'

Stavros explains to his cousin, who listens wide eyed. He finishes by saying, 'You don't know with some of these girls. They look sweet and innocent, but don't trust them. They're promiscuous and will sleep with anyone.'

Both of them shake their heads, and ponder on the iniquities of women.

Georgios is a man in his late forties, whose life has followed a path his mother in those awful years of the second world war had never envisaged. The Germans came and occupied the land. They shot his mother's brother. Georgios was born. Behind the cottage oranges grew, as they had done for years. His father caught fish from the small wooden boat that lay moored, when not in the bay, by the short concrete jetty at the north end of the beach. The war ended and Georgios grew. The family, the brothers and sisters, cousins, aunts and uncles, picked oranges and ate fish. A harbour was built at Tiryns, and in time the tourists came. Now, his mother and father are dead. The old cottage has gone, replaced by a block of apartments; 'Apartments Georgios' the large blue sign proclaims. The Villa Diana on the beach, built by his uncle, is his too. Georgios also owns one of the gift shops in the high street, and has a share in his brother's souvlaki restaurant.

Generally, he is a happy man, except when bothered by the tourists, such as his anglo-saxon namesake, and that man's wife. So, the cat had died. It was old. It is true that it was unfortunate that it had chosen to die where it did, and he probably had not been particularly wise to brick the animal up inside. Still, the Englishman had insisted, and his wife, apparently, had been close to murder. The fact at this moment, however, is that the bloated, festering corpse behind the breeze blocks is now smelling so badly that even the diners at the taverna next door are beginning to sniff the air and poke suspiciously at their stiffadoes. 'Do something,' his wife had told him loudly, a declaration that had carried across the early morning, to the harbour on the right, and to Coronisi in front, and caused more than one eyebrow to be lifted in nearby houses.

Georgios had muttered, and he mutters now. He is not alone. Jo Bullock stands to one side, and Kostas the fisherman on the other. They are a couple of metres away from the breeze-blocks and consider the problem. 'In fact,' Georgios says in English, 'it was right to build a wall, there.' The other two watch him. 'The house is better with the wall,' he continues. 'Yes, but the stench, the smell,' Jo Bullock says and holds his nose. 'The cat stinks, Georgios.'

'OK. OK. It stinks.'

Kostas remembers a rabbit rotting out on Aphrodite, swollen head and gut, eyes decomposed, and smelling of corruption. Georgios was an idiot to have bricked up the cat, and he tells him so. 'You should have taken it to the dump,' Kostas says loudly in Greek.

'Alexos was going to.'

'Then why didn't he?'

'He went to Athens.'

'Why did he go to Athens?'

'I don't know. How should I know why he went to Athens?'

Jo Bullock looks from one to the other, alarmed by the loud and sharp exchange. He is lost, not knowing whether they are arguing or merely exchanging information. 'My opinion is,' he says, 'that you knock down some of the blocks. There, for example. Or there. Go in, get the cat, and dump it. End of problem.' Both Greeks stare at him, amazed. 'Why break the wall?' Georgios demands, bemused. 'Why? I just made the damn thing.'

'Because the cat stinks, Georgios,' Jo says reasonably.

'OK, OK. It stinks, but next week it's finished. No more smell.'

'But next week I'll be in Basingstoke,' Jo says, shocked. 'England.'

'OK, OK,' Georgios counters. 'England.'

'But what about now?' Jo says, agitated. 'Now, Georgios, now.' Georgios considers the present, and shrugs his shoulders. Next week the man will be gone, most of this lot will be gone. New people will come, and if the smell is still there no one will know what it comes from. He shrugs his shoulders with greater certainty. 'OK,' he says.

'No, not OK,' Jo replies with undisguised despair. Georgios sucks his teeth and reaches in the pockets of his old brown trousers for his cigarettes. It is OK and he knows it's OK. In time the smell will go away, the tourists will go away, and in winter, in the mornings and afternoons and evenings, the beach will be empty.

He smiles at the Englishman and says, 'OK.'

The girl and boy lie quietly on their beds, reading. A fan, bought for twenty pounds on their first day, hums quietly on the small bedside table in the room which their parents share. The doors between the two rooms are open. The glass doors that lead from each bedroom onto the balcony are also open. Only the two bedside lights in the children's room are on. Jo Bullock sits on the end of his own bed, and rubs his hands together. His watch alarm goes off. It is eleven o'clock. The full moon is high above Coronisi; the disc is clear and the seas quite visible. It shines down on Tiryns, a great glowing orange globe which lights up shimmering patches of water, and reveals dark shadows of boats pulling at their moorings.

Jo Bullock eyes the quiet, passive forms of his children, and then recoils at the awful loneliness that occupies the strange silence in the small, dour apartment. He stares out at the balcony, at a corner of chair and table, and the lank fall of drying towels on the railings. Mary has gone again, and her absence is a dead weight. He gets up and goes onto the balcony, looks up at the moon and the light it throws across the water, and then stares down the beach, into nothing, hoping desperately that she is not with that man again, but knowing too well that she is.

A bottle of ouzo stands on the table, next to a glass and a jug of water. He pours himself a glass, adds water and swirls the white liquid round and round before drinking. 'Dad?' His son calls quietly, and calls again. 'Go to sleep,' he tells him. 'Where's Mum?' Jo doesn't answer. The girl gets up and goes to the bathroom, and says nothing. The abyss of silence between the children and the parents is a day to day fact. The children have long ago absorbed this daily emptiness, hiding it away inside themselves. It is a wordless chasm that each member of the family knows about, but none dares face. The girl comes back to bed. She has changed into her nightdress, and holds it by each side as she steps carefully across the floor. Her father watches, and sees the movement of a child beyond his reach. The boy follows her to the bathroom and soon returns. Their light goes out.

Jo Bullock walks across the room. The ouzo is

thick on his tongue, and claws in his stomach. As he reaches the door and opens it he hears the beds move, and a murmur of words.

The man's name is Vassilis, and though Jo Bullock knows nothing about him it is enough that he is with Mary. In many ways, in spite of the anger, the jealousy, and though he does not admit to it readily, in spite of the shame, he does not want to know about this Greek intruder in his life. He does not want to know about his house or his wife or his children. The fact that he knows his name is an intrusion, and he would just as soon that he had never heard it. He goes down the stairs and onto the beach. The moon is to his left. It is ten minutes before he covers the distance from their villa to the main beach; he walks quickly and only slows down when he nears the Villa Diana. The tavernas that stretch along this part of the beach, almost up to The Delphi, are still full. Bouzouki music comes down from the loudspeakers hung up in the vines that cover the trelliswork which climbs up the crude cement walls, or is stretched above the heads of the diners like a false ceiling. He searches the shadows restlessly, his body agitated by reflexes he cannot control. Awkwardly, he peers into alleyways, and he kicks stupidly at large stones and rough pieces of old concrete; and then seconds later he is down by the water, unsuccessfully trying to avoid the waves as the sea moves up and down the beach. From time to time he wanders up and down the main street, where lights blaze and shops are still open. Greek Art. Soft overblown peaches. Old men, standing in doorway with their white vests and black belted trousers. Taxis in from Nafplion. Heads bent low over three hundred drachma souvlakis. Jo notices what he has already seen so often, but registers little.

He finds them just after midnight, sitting on the harbour wall, legs hanging over. He comes closer. They are talking. The fact that Mary obviously enjoys talking to this total stranger is something that he does not know how to deal with. Mary is a distant person, but over the years he has convinced himself that he knows her. She is intelligent. She is pretty. He likes that in her. It is good to have a pretty wife. He stands at one end of the harbour wall, hidden in the shadows. By keeping close to the brickwork he finds that he can edge closer to where the two are sitting. He stops as he hears them laugh aloud. Mary's laugh is sharp and brittle, and it unnerves him. Why is she laughing? What are they talking about? The voices rise and fall. Jo stares at the water in the harbour beneath him. What in God's name does she find to say to the Greek?

The question has no answer, because it is not a question; it is a lament.

Later, he lies awake in bed, and at five in the morning he is joined by his wife, who tiptoes into the room, past the silent, poised, alert faces of her two children, and then round to the bed. For an hour or two they sleep, and in his dreams Jo Bullock falls endlessly into an ever descending pit.

TUESDAY

Soon we go home. The feeling of something about to happen here in Tiryns is almost oppressive. 'Something is about to happen,' I said to George, wanting to talk to him. He was standing naked in the doorway of the bathroom. The sun has done little to make poor George a more attractive figure. He will soon be fat. 'Thank God for that,' was all I got as a reply. How is it that a man with his responsibilities can be so flippant? It's as though he feels the English language is not the proper vehicle for serious conversation, and so he banters on and on and drives me mad. So I didn't tell him what that old vulture down in The Delphi had seen, but I did tell Ann Preston.

She was down on the beach, just as people were beginning to clear away their towels and umbrellas at the end of the day. I didn't notice her at first. I'd been at the far end, near The Delphi, and had stopped momentarily to watch four young men throw a volleyball, one to the other, again and again, hard and accurate. They were earnest, determined young men I'd noticed several times before, strong and well built, whose perfect faces would break every now and again with laughter. I watched the ball, and the bodies jump, climb out of the water, and then arch as the fist slammed down, sending the ball back across the water, so hard that it took the catcher with it, back and over, to vanish for some seconds amidst a huge kickback of spray. They laughed, and I smiled, and as I did so I saw Ann Preston standing not far away and, like me, watching.

'Come and have a drink,' she said. I went upstairs to her flat. It's like ours, bare and basic. Clothes were everywhere, across the beds, on the floor, piled on the chairs. Half a water melon, chopped at with a knife, was covered with sand on the floor by the fridge. An opened tub of yoghurt sat on a table next to a snorkel. 'The boys', she said, indicating the mess. She gave me a gin and tonic. She smokes. I said I used to but didn't now. I felt awkward, and knew I shouldn't. She has clear, radiant skin, but her eyes are wild. They move restlessly, and I felt them penetrate me. I told her about Harriet Simmons and said, 'You know her binoculars?' She nodded. 'How she uses them all the time?'

'It's the other woman who can see,' Ann said. 'I think Harriet Simmons is as blind as a bat.' The observation made me wonder, and made some sense of that relationship. 'Well, anyway,' I said, 'they've spotted them, those young men. They're back.' Ann looked at me quickly, her eyes intense, drawn on mine. 'Yes,' I insisted, 'they're back. Here.'

'Where?'

'There.' I pointed at Aphrodite.

'On the island?'

'Yes.'

She laughed at that and said, 'Well, why not? It wouldn't be right without them, would it? I mean, they belong as much as, well, you and me.' She coughed, and the cough was coarse and vulgar, and that broke the spell of the woman, and I felt myself relax. We talked about the young men, and wondered what had happened, how they had got away from the police, and what had made them climb the tower that night at Epidavrus. Then we talked about poor Jo Bullock and his attempt at organising us, and then we talked about his wife. I said, 'What is she up to?' And Ann said if the woman wanted the Greek then she couldn't see why not and that her husband was a bore. 'And that's sufficient reason?' I insisted. God, who taught me such morality? 'It's a reason,' she said, and her eyes were set, so that I looked away. We had another drink. The beach cleared for a few minutes. Below us a waiter scraped at the sand with a rake. Am I wrong or is the smell from the cat a little better than yesterday? Or are we just getting used to it? 'I don't know,' I said, wanting to talk. 'Maybe you're right. I mean, you come to a place like this for two weeks, maybe more, and nothing that you've ever done in your life really makes sense here. The rules are different. It's a different game.'

'On Friday she'll get on the bus, and go to Athens,' Ann said. 'And that will be the end of it.'

'Will they talk about it?' I asked. 'I mean, when they get home.' The question worried me, but I had to ask it. 'Why should they?' she said confidently. And then she told me about her children, and her marriage, and she told me that she watched other women with their men, and felt rage and envy. So I told her that I was tired of George, and tired of that creep down at the office, and that I wanted a life I would never have. And then I found her looking at me strangely. I asked her why and she said, 'Your husband.'

'Yes?' I was startled.

'It's just that you surprise me,' she said. I didn't know what to say then, and she went on to say, 'Because I find him a very attractive man.' That threw me, and it still does. I hear voices in my head, over and over again. She meant it. I laughed, a short nervous laugh, which I hated myself for because it was a stupid reaction. 'Really?' I said, weakly. 'George? Good God.'

She nodded. 'Yes.'

So, I have sat here tonight knowing that she has been watching my husband, and so, of course, has Maeve.

There are lights on Aphrodite. For the first time since we arrived. They mark the place where the young men have put up a tent. The lights flicker. They are burning wood.

EIGHT

On the night of the second Wednesday Julia finds herself with James and Elaine Moss at the bar of The Ship. The bar itself has recently been remodelled and Dimitris is proud of the mirrored backdrop and the coloured lights in the false wooden ceiling. The stereo plays Womack and Womack and Elaine Moss moves back and forwards on her stool to the beat. She wears a light blue skirt and a white silk top that barely meets across her breasts. Blue bangles clatter on her wrists as she plays with her glass.

Elaine Moss is drinking her second Tequila Sunrise. James Moss stands next to her, and she tells him he looks like someone out of the Next Directory. He doesn't dispute it. Reflecting on unspoken memories he drinks his second Harvey Wallbanger. 'Tomorrow,' he says conspiratorially to Julia, 'we'll do the lot.'

'What lot?' Julia asks, perplexed.

'The lot we haven't done,' Elaine explains. She points at the list of cocktails which Dimitris displays beside the bar.

'Forty seven cocktails,' Dimitris says proudly. 'Forty eight if you count the Dimitris Special.'

'What's that?' Julia asks, confused.

'He doesn't know,' Elaine says. 'Do you, Dimitris? The owner grins. He thrives on familiarity. Julia watches them. She sees Elaine Moss flirting quite openly, and her husband standing by, seemingly quite happy about it. 'They're crazy,' Dimitris says to Julia, indicating the young couple. 'Drink like fish. Tequila, vodka, gin, campari, whisky, bourbon, beer.'

'We don't do beer, Dimitris,' Elaine chides him.

'OK, so no beer.'

'You mean you've tried all that stuff?' Julia asks, indicating the list of cocktails, and genuinely horrified. James Moss nods. 'Forty of them. So far.'

'We'll do the rest tomorrow, won't we, James?' Elaine says friskily. James sucks in through his teeth and says, 'Yup.'

'Why?' Julia asks.

'Because,' James tells her, 'a good cocktail is what a holiday is all about, really, when you think about it.'

Julia confesses that she hasn't quite thought about it in that way before.

'Listen,' Dimitris says. 'You pay eight hundred, a thousand, twelve hundred drachs.' 'Maybe more,' Elaine says, interrupting, her voice suddenly high. 'OK, maybe more,' Dimitris comes back quickly, ' but what the hell, it's a good drink. I make the best damn cocktail in Tiryns.'

'You make the best damn cocktail in Greece,' Elaine screams, exploding with laughter. The couple drain their drinks. 'Come on, Julia,' Elaine says, reaching out with her hand, 'don't be so glum. Drink up. Where's George?' George, Julia believes, is with Maeve. 'God knows,' she replies. 'Then have a drink,' Elaine says.

'No, thanks,' Julia declines. 'I don't seem to have your capacity.'

'When I met James,' Elaine says, face glowing, hand on Julia's arm, 'I was drinking a Rusty Nail in a bar on Poros. Great big one it was, like this. I was talking to a guy from Manchester. Only drank beer. Suddenly, there was this banging and grunting from inside the Men's. Of course, we all stopped talking to see what it was. Bang, bang, and we could see the door shaking as though something was trying to get out. "Christ," I said, "what's that?" And this guy I was talking to, the one from Manchester, said, "Oh, that's only my mate. He's probably pissed." Well, I didn't doubt that. Seconds later the door was flung open and this wild-eyed maniac came flying into the bar, his face just like a vampire. Well, any normal person would've keeled over, I mean, he was that pissed. But he didn't. He just stood there, leaning on the bar, and said, "Barman, give us a Kiss In The

Dark." Well, that was it. I just cracked up.' Julia decides she ought to respond, but is not quite sure how to. She opts for, 'So what happened to that wretched young man?'

'Why, I married him, of course.'

Julia's attention turns to the street outside, which is now livening up for the early part of the evening as campers come in to the supermarkets and the early barhoppers start on their first drinks. The bus from Nafplion blasts its horn. It is answered by another set of blasts from a German tourist trying to manoeuvre his Mercedes into a space that not even a small Fiat could have negotiated. Greeks gather and speculate on the sanity of the German. One old man spits on the ground; his brother had been shot dead one night against a wall in Crete during the war. Marched out of the back door and shot without a word. And here was another damn German trying to go where any half intelligent human being with eyes in his head could tell that he wasn't wanted. The Mercedes scratches a Lancia, and an Italian rushes out of the nearby supermarket, screaming. The German examines the scratch, and notices that he is the centre of attention. Julia and the two Mosses stand with Dimitris in the doorway of The Ship. The bus driver blasts the horn again. He grins, and waves at Fat Spyros who saunters up the street. Spyros approaches the German and the Italian. The Italian gesticulates wildly. In his right hand he holds a toilet roll, part of his unfinished shopping. The owner of the supermarket stands in his doorway, eyeing the unpaid for article. The bus is to one side of the street, the Lancia the other. The front of the Mercedes is half a metre down between the two. A deep scratch is already apparent on the paintwork of the Lancia's offside. It is also quite clear that any attempt to move the Mercedes will result in further damage.

James Moss laughs openly, a deep belly laugh that makes the Italian stop and the German turn in disbelief. 'It is not so funny,' the German protests.

'You should come and stand where I'm standing,' James Moss tells him. Julia sniggers and sidles off, but as she goes she is restrained. She turns, surprised to see Martin Rushton. 'Let's sit and watch,' he says, 'and drink to Europe.'

Martin Rushton has not been feeling very good for some time. The two weeks in Tiryns have done much to unsettle his confidence. He is convinced, finally, that he is not a European. He does not feel European, and he does not think European. Sitting on the balcony of his room at The Delphi, with Maeve absent, no doubt in hot pursuit of that dissolute headmaster, he tells himself that on the contrary he is Anglo-Saxon and thinks like an Anglo-Saxon. He mourns the loss of fahrenheit and ounces. He thinks proudly of Trafalgar and Blenheim, and he revels in the defeat of Montcalm and Dupleix. He drinks Glenfiddich, which he has bought at a price from the liquor shop, and he belches scorn at the thought of demestica, ouzo and metaxa. 'Bugger them all,' he whispers.

'Bugger them all,' he says again, and savours the scotch. He should never have given in to Maeve's artful persuasiveness, and her desire to research the morals of the British holidaymaker on the beaches of Greece. It was not something, he should have told her, that needed research. And how is it, he wonders, that where Hamburg, Vienna, Paris and Madrid, the Alps and the coasts of Spain had for years failed to raise no more than a ghost of a suspicion, this small town, white and dry at the head of the Argolic Bay, has made him realise just how little he really knows of Europe? Tiryns has caught him unawares. Enmeshed in this two week time warp the old stereotypes return to haunt him. The Italians scream and shout, wear designer T-shirts and flex their muscles on the beach; the French are a ragbag of mouth-pursing garrulous curiosities, who move in groups, totally lost in the context of non-Gallic surroundings; the Germans are everywhere, know everything, and have lots of money - Ah Italy, yes the last time I was in your country I was driving my tank; the Austrians put cream on their eggs and yodel in their baths; the Archimedes Screw was the old Greek term for buggery; the British lie in the sun and get drunk. As he drinks another whisky these old references taunt him, but in time, and as the sun goes down over Aphrodite he relaxes and stops fighting back. Like someone nurtured too long on vegetarian food and wholemeal bread who dines one night in ecstasy on blood red meat and the whitest of breads, he sucks in contentment, and his body registers a shudder of unfamiliar pleasure.

Sudden seriousness enters his now drink inspired face. 'Fuck it, anyway,' he announces. 'I'm damned if I'm going to give up a decent living. What, give up the company, just because of my fucking conscience? I'd have to be fucking mad. Got to earn a crust, haven't we? I'll be a European as long as it pays. I'll facilitate all those silly bastards right up their arseholes. Fuck them.' And as an afterthought, he adds, 'And fuck Andreas. Bloody Greek.'

Wandering up the main street a while later, Martin witnesses the altercation between the German, the Italian, and the local bus, sees Fat Spyros approach to exercise his normal role as mediator in such events, and spies Julia Moore in the doorway of The Ship. 'Have a drink,' he says, his hand briefly touching her arm. They sit down at one of the tables on the street. 'Carnival,' he says.

'There's no way back. No way forwards,' she comments.

'Gin and tonic?' he suggests.

'Lovely.'

He orders a beer for himself, and they watch the Mosses stroll away. 'That young couple are seriously twisted,' Martin says. 'She told me that in total she has drunk about one hundred cocktails since arriving here. That's nearly ten a day. That's,' and he counts, 'about forty pounds a day. Just for her alone. They're crazy.'

Fat Spyros grins at the German and the Italian and then talks to the bus driver. Their conversation is a harmony of declamation, a polyphony from the road and the driver's seat.

The passengers in the bus get off, and watch. On the pavement the Italian shakes the toilet roll at old Nicos, from the supermarket. Incredibly, the bus begins to roll forward, missing by a hair's breadth the shops on one side and leaving the Mercedes free on the other. The German looks on helplessly.

Dimitris watches the movement with pride and

says, 'What a driver. Spyros' brother, the bus driver.' A few seconds later he adds, 'my cousin.' But Martin is thinking of Maeve and says to Julia, 'You see, when Maeve gets an idea into her head she won't give up. She's convinced that George, your husband, is, well,...'

'Oh, God,' Julia says before she can stop herself. 'Interesting?'

'Precisely.'

She sips at the gin and tonic and eyes Martin over the glass. 'Well, I suppose it's a compliment. Probably is.' She laughs nervously. 'You should ask her to talk to me. I mean, I do know something about him. He's totally amoral, you know.'

'He can't be. He's a headmaster.'

'He doesn't have moral standards. Not normal ones, anyway.'

Martin drinks his beer, and then says, 'What's he doing? I mean, now.'

'I imagine that rather depends on your wife,' Julia answers, forcing a smile.

The bus clears the Mercedes and the Lancia, and Fat Spyros wanders off. The German and the Italian are still locked together. 'You drive,' the German says. 'That way.'

'Why?' the Italian demands. 'Why me? You drive.'

Martin registers truth settling over him. 'I think I've just become a heretic,' he says. And then adds, 'What are you going to do now? I mean, tonight.'

'The Mosses asked me to go up to Cavos with them.'

'The disco? They're all twelve years old.'

'I don't give a damn,' Julia replies. 'Not tonight, anyway.'

Julia Moore has two Dimitris Specials with the Mosses. Dimitris is reluctant to tell her what they contain, or even what makes them so many shades of blue. 'You change the ingredients, don't you, Dimitris?' Elaine says. Dimitris remains silent. Whatever the cocktails consist of Julia registers a significant fraying of her perception of the real world. People in her immediate vicinity move in and out of direct vision like ghosts, insubstantial forms that ape the antics of human life, hesitate before her and then pass on into the night. That bastard, George, is out there somewhere with that witch, Maeve. Julia Moore leans against the bar and gouges runnels of blood from Maeve's face. She ties her to a stake and lights piles of dry brush and crackling twigs. Maeve twists and screams, a demon dying.

'What's on your mind?' Dimitris asks.

'I was thinking about England,' Julia says. Inspired, she continues, 'my cat.'

'You have a cat?' Dimitris' eyes are wide. He wonders about this woman's husband, how free she might be, and then remembers that he has seen the man and that woman who writes for magazines buying nectarines from Spyros' shop. 'I have a cat,' he says, remembering that it is a line that has served him well in the past.

'Actually, I don't have a cat,' Julia says. She had always wanted a cat. There had once been a kitten but it had fallen foul of the neighbour's dog. 'I had a kitten, but it never made it.'

'Maybe you should get an early night,' Dimitris suggests. 'I could walk you home.'

Julia considers the suggestion, and then says, 'I'm going to the disco.' She slides off her stool. The Mosses go with her. Together they climb the dusty track that leads to Cavos. There are several discos in Tiryns, but this is the largest, the loudest and the most expensive. The Mosses go there nightly, the final destination on their round of the bars, the last refuge from the growing fear that the perfect cocktail may not really exist. Noise from the disco rolls down the hill towards them. Stray beams of light, blue, green and red, leap out into the dark. People, all young, pass them, in pairs or small groups. Julia sees a familiar face, staring at her in genuine dismay. It is Gail, who shakes her head, urging her mother away, but Julia is too confused by Dimitris' cocktails to register the reason for her daughter's alarm, and moves on. However, at the disco entrance she loses the Mosses and finds herself alone. She is surprised at first, then panics. She looks about her, and wonders what she is doing here, in this dress, in this place, alone. Shadows move. One of them approaches. Of course she knows him, and smiles. 'Remember me? Stavros?'

'Hullo, Stavros?'

'Are you OK, Mrs Moore?'

'Julia. Julia. Yes, I'm fine.'

'OK. Julia. I like that. I had a friend once, called Julia.' And so he had, several of them.

'Really?' She struggles with the thought of this other Julia while registering that Stavros has moved closer to her.

'What are you doing?' he asks. She denies all knowledge of the disco. 'Just walking,' she tells him. 'Just walking? That's nice. I like walking. Do you want an ice-cream?' The disco stands on the hill above the bay, and Julia Moore looks down on the serene silence that lies out at sea, beyond the lights. The absurdity of the enquiry appeals to her. An ice cream? Why not? She follows him

down the track, catching at his hand to prevent
herself from slipping. Stavros has a motorbike,
and she climbs up behind him, holding on tightly to
his waist as he manoeuvres the machine through
the crowds. They go down among the new
buildings that have risen by the road that leads out
to Assini, and then out of town, rising higher as the
roads climbs round the cliff. Julia holds on tight,
vaguely wondering where he is taking her.

When they stop Tiryns is below them and to the
right, nearly two kilometres away. By the side of
the road Julia sees a small villa. 'Come,' Stavros
tells her. She follows him, past some upturned
empty beer crates, and down a narrow path that
leads to a door. 'Come,' he repeats. He smiles.
She follows. When he reaches the door she stands
behind him. As the door opens she sees a bare
room. She stands quite still, hearing a dog barking
loudly. An icon hangs on a wall, red and blue and
gold and shining out on the emptiness of the room.
The walls are white and peeling. A naked bulb
hangs from a flex in the centre of the ceiling.
Against the far wall, and under the icon, is a bed,
without blankets, covered by a white sheet.

Julia hears the dog barking, and listens to its
voice as it echoes down the dry slopes towards
Tiryns.

'I don't want any ice-cream,' she whispers, but

her voice is low and drowned by the howling of the lone mongrel that wonders among the rocks of old Assini.

THURSDAY

It is now early morning of the final Thursday. Tomorrow night, Friday, we board the bus for Athens. There is one more day, here in Tiryns, and one more night. Next Monday I will open the door of Dixon and Brown and wait at my desk for him to come in, breathing heavily, Lawrence Brown, puffing as he pulls off his heavy black coat, puffing as he assiduously wipes his shiny black shoes on the mat at the door. That heavy body will then roll across the room. I'll watch his face light up, those blue eyes crinkle. I'll feel his stubby, overfleshed hands fall lightly on my arm, and he'll bend down, and use the absence of two weeks from his office as excuse enough to press his damp lips against my cheek.

Or, I will not go to the office. I will stay at home. But what about the money? I know the argument. We need the money. There must be other jobs, but then I haven't got the training. And training costs money, which we haven't got.

Last night was long. I was with the Mosses and we drank Dimitris' Specials. Martin is right. That young couple are truly crazy. Then they went to the disco and I went for a walk, down by the new pizza houses and open bars, the red plastic and the Germans and the Swiss and the Austrians, past the camp sites and up the road that goes to ancient Assini. And somewhere I stopped. There was a dog, crawling among the stones, and every now and again it barked. I stood there for a long time, watching the shadows, careful of the dog, and then I came back home.

I reached the apartment about two. Both Gail and Tom were in their rooms, asleep. Tom's door was open and I could hear him move restlessly under the sheet. Carefully, I lit a mosquito coil and put it by his bed, and then I came back to our room. George was still out. With her, of course. I lay down on the bed, and listened to the sea. I spent the next hour fitfully, half asleep, sometimes sitting up, and at one stage I found myself actually out of bed, on the balcony. And I began to reconstruct the evening. I had met Stavros on the road as I was walking up to Assini and he had offered me a lift on his bike, which I accepted. And then he asked if I wanted to stop for a coffee or an ice-cream. I told him I didn't like ice cream, and that I was tired, and so he brought me back home.

I said good night, got off the bike, and walked down the narrow lane to the Villa Diana.

When Julia gets home George is apparently still out and the children are asleep. She sits on the bed and thinks of her husband with Maeve. 'Damn you, George,' she says in a whisper. 'Damn you, damn you.' She stands up and walks out to the balcony. 'Why her?' The question is uttered aloud. Outside, the sea rolls, and a wind picks up further down the coast; clouds blow up above the islands. She returns to the bed and cries freely, tormented by images of Lawrence Brown, Maeve and George. She cries for the miserable Bullocks. She cries for herself. 'Oh, damn you, George. Where are you?'

She is answered by her son, who says sleepily, 'For God's sake, Mum, you've probably busted in his head with all your jumping up and down. Dad's under the bed.'

Julia hesitates, then moves quickly and peers under the bed where she sees a vague shadow stretched out like a corpse. At one end a quick flutter of white suggests that an eye has opened and closed. 'George!' she hisses. 'Dad's not well,' Tom says. 'Leave him alone, Mum. He'll be OK in the morning.'

'What makes you think he's not so well?' Julia demands, her voice shaking slightly.

'The way he threw up.'
'Damn him,' Julia says, concluding the encounter.

NINE

For the Mosses this particular Thursday opens with a blur. They find themselves lying on their backs on the quayside by the edge of the harbour. They are fully dressed, he in his Next trousers and shirt, she in her silk blouse, skirt and bangles. 'Can't remember a thing,' James admits.

'Me neither.'

'Still. Only seven to go,' he says, yawning, and remembering the untried cocktails in Dimitris' bar. He sits up and his wife follows. Tiryns is already awake. Kostas is out in his boat. A lone pedallo makes its purposeful way out to Coronisi. A gull dives at the early morning sea. On the beach the honey truck rumbles outside Vangelis', sucking out the sewage and belching stench up the alleyways and into the main street. 'I couldn't live here,' Elaine says, flexing her toes. And then she adds with alarm, 'Hey, James?' He looks at her, querying the tone in her voice. 'Where are my shoes?'

'Christ knows,' he replies. 'And where are yours?' she adds, staring at his naked feet. James shakes his head. His memory, as so often, has left him exposed. 'Guess what?' he says, starting an old game.

'What?'

'One dash of orange bitters, two measures gin, one measure dry vermouth. Go on, guess.'

'Easy. Astoria. I know that one alright. An Astoria.' She is pleased and grins at him. 'OK. My turn. One half measure lemon juice. One half measure Cointreau. One measure gin.' He purses his lips. 'No problem, Elaine. White Lady.' 'Now this one,' she says quickly, determined to get him. 'The other way round. OK?' He nods. 'Bobby Burns.' She laughs aloud, certain that this will beat him. 'It's got to be a scotch,' he says. 'Uh, uh.' 'With vermouth?' 'Oh, clever boy,' she says and claps her hands. He grins and answers 'then I've got it. One measure sweet vermouth. One measure scotch. Three dashes of Benedictine.'

Elaine narrows her eyes and then leans across and puts her arms round her husband. 'I adore you, James,' she tells him. James smiles back at his wife. He loves her too. Only once has he caught her out, and that was with Dubonnet Fizz. She'd forgotten to mention that it needed the juice of quarter of a lemon. 'Let's take the boat out,' she says with sudden decisiveness. At the beginning of the holiday on impulse and after a Brandy Alexander they had spent twenty thousand drachmas on a rubber dinghy that was big enough to take both of them. For another few thousand drachmas the shopowner, Dimitris' cousin Vangelis, had given them a pair of oars. So, they have the boat which, for one reason and another, maybe, James had on one occasion reflected, it was because they had never had another Brandy Alexander, they had never used, not even once.

'Where do you want to go?' James asks her.

'There,' she says, pointing at Aphrodite. 'I'll get some mixes, a bottle of gin, some rum. We'll make a few, then go back to Dimitris' at lunch to start on the rest.'

'What about food?' He wonders.

Elaine looks at her husband. 'OK. We'll go back to the flat and I'll make you some cornflakes.'

'Thanks,' he says appreciatively. 'Sure you don't mind?'

An hour and a half later the Mosses descend to the beach from their flat. She carries a bag. He carries the boat. They reach the water's edge and hesitate. Christos, who runs one of the small pedallo units on the beach notices them and stops his game of chess. He sees them push the boat out and clamber in. He hears the bottles crash against each other, and watches the young man clumsily take the oars. They move slowly away from shore. The morning is clear and there is no wind. He shrugs his shoulders and returns to his game of chess. On her balcony, Harriet Simmons sweeps her binoculars along the beach and notices the small grey dinghy move away from the shoreline. 'There's that young man and his pretty young wife,' she says to Betty. Betty hears nothing; she is asleep in her chair. 'And now she's taking off her dress. And her bra.' Harriet's voice is clipped, striking time, disapproving.

On the island of Aphrodite the three young men stand in shorts and T-shirts and drink beer. One of them spies the small grey dinghy being rowed out from Tiryns.

The Mosses drink a mixture of gin and fruit juice, and talk about the seven cocktails at The Ship which they have yet to try. There is some disagreement as to what the final seven actually are, and the discussion is heated. 'Right, one more time,' Elaine says. 'But I've already told you,' he protests. 'No, one more time. Blue Lagoon. Ruby Tuesday. Purple Sundowner. Jackie Kennedy...' 'No, we had the Jackie Kennedy the first Wednesday,' James insists. 'Remember?' 'No, we didn't. That was Mai Tai. Mai Tais and Singapore Sling. I remember it clearly,' she says fiercely, 'and you know I've got a good memory, which is news to him and makes him say, 'You don't even remember the first Wednesday.' She is hurt and says, 'I do so. Mai Tais and Singapore Sling. Oh, why are you arguing with me, James? Why are you arguing with me on our last day?'

'I'm not arguing.'

'Then why say it's not a Jackie Kennedy when it is? One more time, OK? Blue Lagoon. Ruby Tuesday. Purple Sundowner. Jackie Kennedy.' And then she stops and stares at the bottom of the dinghy. 'James? James, there's water coming into the boat. There, at the bottom. By your feet.'

He stares at the water, then looks in panic at his wife. 'Quick, bail!'

'Bail? What do you mean, bail?'

'With the jug. The jug, quick!'

'But it's full of gin, you idiot!'

James Moss hesitates and looks keenly at the young woman he had married, now half naked, red shouldered. 'You're crazy!' he shouts. 'We're sinking, for Christ's sake, and I can't swim!'

On the island the three young men wade into the water. They hesitate, watching the boat sink lower, and then two of them strike out towards it, swimming fast. The third one, his arm helpless in plaster, shakes his head. They reach the boat as it disappears. They find Elaine Moss holding on to an oar, gasping for breath. Her husband has disappeared. One of the men swims off in search of the missing husband; the other tries to pull the helpless woman to shore, but she is heavy and does not cooperate. She slips away from him, and when nearly two minutes later they find her again she is unconscious and full of water. The man is lost. Slowly, they pull the woman to the island, and lie her down on the pebble beach. 'She's dead,' one of them says. 'Didn't have a chance.'

'She isn't dead,' the one in plaster pronounces.

One of the two who had gone to rescue her starts to pump up and down on her front. The other pulls her head back and tries to revive her by blowing into her mouth. They keep this up endlessly, on and on, till finally a steady trickle of blue and red and yellow liquid bubbles up and swirls out of her mouth, before dripping down on to the pebbles.

On the balcony of the Hotel Delphi Harriet Simmons searches the bay with her binoculars, and when she reaches the beach of Aphrodite she hesitates, and gasps. 'Oh, my God! What animals!.' Betty takes the binoculars from her and concentrates on what her companion has seen. 'Dear God,' she joins in. 'First one on top of her and then another.' Her voice shakes with emotion. 'Disgusting, filthy animals.'

'Who is it?' Harriet demands. 'Who? What

kind of woman would let herself do a thing like that?'

'She's probably a German. Or an Austrian,' Betty says.

'Well, I don't know, I don't know,' Harriet continues, plainly distressed. 'But I do think it's disgusting. And in daylight, too.' Betty stares at her companion. A moment of revulsion grips her, as she thinks of the constant misery of having to endlessly fawn and scrape to this woman. And yet, this emotion won't do. Tomorrow they go back to England; the future terrifies her. 'Quite,' she says. 'Absolutely disgusting.'

Back on the island the young men stare down at the dead woman. They agree they should not leave her there, and without further discussion lift her up and take her out into the sea, where, at a distance of nearly one hundred metres, they let her go.

On the Thursday evening Tom tells his parents he is going snorkelling in the harbour. 'Squid and stuff,' he tells them. 'Wannanoctopus, Mum?'

'No,' she tells him firmly.

'Only asked.'

'I heard you.' Julia lies on her bed, trying to sleep. 'Careful of the currents,' George tells him. 'Go with him, George,' Julia urges. George closes his eyes, and Tom escapes, mask, flippers and snorkel clutched tightly in his hands. 'Then you go, Gail,' Julia tries again, calling out to her daughter. Gail sits silently in front of the mirror in her room and applies lipstick. Like her father, she decides to ignore the request. 'Everybody's deaf,' Julia announces. She is answered by continued silence. 'He could drown,' Julia points out. A fly settles on the ceiling above her, and she stares at it. The fly's head grows large, spreading across the plaster, a head, a face, a smile she knows only too well. Quite suddenly she leaps in the air and smashes at the fly with her open hand.

'For Christ's sake, Mum!' Gail rushes into the room and stares at her parents, at her father sitting bolt upright on the bed, eyes wide open as he focuses on his wife, and at her mother as she brings a fly splattered hand down from the ceiling. Mesmerised by her own violence Julia stares into the palm of her hand, examining the blood and brains of Lawrence Brown. 'What in the hell was that all about?' George demands. 'A fly,' she answers quietly. Gail continues to stare at her mother, and then says finally, 'Did you have to?'

Julia walks across to the bathroom. 'it reminded me of something. Or other.' She says at last.

Tom would have been curious to examine the contents of Lawrence Brown's head, but as it is he is ignorant of his mother's attack on the fly, and quite taken up by his own activities. The harbour wall, or more precisely the part of the wall below the water, has fascinated him since he discovered it at the end of the first week. It is a jungle of strange forms, rich waving fronds, broken glass and old cans, huge sea cucumbers, pink and red anemones, fish, still and hardly visible behind stems of weed. It is a mass of concrete, cracked and broken into a rough surface, crossed by small crevices, overgrown in places by soft algae. It is, at times, a sudden luminous space, a great cavern of shining water through which he must swim alone, like an astronaut cut off from life, floating in space. He dives and passes along the harbour wall, examining stem by stem the moving weed, the frightened fish, the still dark forms of glass bottles. His eyes are wide behind the mask. His fingers splay open. His feet move gently. He dives, and kicks against the water, forcing himself down to the bottom. He clutches with his fingers at the rocks, and then comes up for air. He goes down again, right to the bottom, and follows a rope that at one, far, distant end, is attached to a fishing vessel. The rope is slack and twists and turns across the seafloor. It moves out from the wall, and then back. He stops, hands out in front. His eyes grow behind the mask. Air escapes from his mouth so that he pushes the tube back quickly behind his lips.

He is face to face with a woman. She is almost naked. Her hair is long and floats about her face. The rope is twisted round one leg so that she cannot move. He moves closer and pulls the hair from her face, and knows then who it is. Seconds later he is on the surface and swimming quickly for the beach. He hauls himself out of the water and pulls of the flippers and mask. He has seen a body. A dead person. He looks up and down the beach, then back to the harbour.

The evening closes in quickly. When he gets home he avoids his mother and sister, and finds his father on the balcony drinking ouzo. 'Dad?' His voice is urgent. George looks up. 'Dad, I saw something.'

'Go and have a shower,' his father tells him.

Tom remembers the dead woman's face and says again, 'Dad. It's important.' George Moore watches his son start to cry, sees the familiar face suddenly troubled, and is perplexed by the tears that stream down the boy's face.

'What is it?' George asks, but Tom shakes his head and runs from the balcony.
The group sits down to a final dinner together on the beach outside The Ship, unaware that the

Mosses, though obviously missing, are dead. Andreas has been a vague figure to most of them, a large imposing man, with a taste for expensive clothes and, rumour generally has it, a great deal of money. Beyond that no one claims greater knowledge. There are some, like Terry and Dina, who only now realise that he is the owner of the agency which organised their holiday. 'Top dog,' Terry says about Andreas to his wife. 'Big bouzouki player.' 'He doesn't play the bouzouki,' she points out sharply. Terry reaches out for the bread and knows that tonight there is going to be another argument. In an hour or two, no more than that, her voice will become even sharper, and the comments even wilder.

'I didn't say he did,' he tells her.

'You said he was a big bouzouki player.'

'I also said he was top dog. Doesn't mean he gets taken walkies every morning.'

'You're a smart mouth, Terry Peters.'

'All I said was he's a big shot.'

'He's off again,' Dina says to Ann Preston, nodding at her husband. 'Don't know why I put up with him.' Terry sucks his teeth and drinks demestica. 'I could get used to this stuff,' he says to the table at large. Andreas, at the end of the table, listens. 'I couldn't,' Martin Rushton says, replying to Terry's comment. He sits back in his chair and registers unease. The prospect of another meal, more lamb, more beans, more feta cheese, more tomatoes and more olive oil, dismays him. He reaches for Maeve's hand, and she turns, silently questioning him. 'Next year,' he whispers, suggesting other places, and Maeve nods, and smiles at George Moore. Andreas catches George and Maeve looking at each other. This man and this woman are like so many others he has seen before. Marionettes, and yet with a strange and touching belief in their own destiny. He wonders if it is only the Anglo-Saxons whose conceit leads them to believe they can actually control the future. He draws back from this group of Britons, the Greenbaums and the Moores, this woman journalist and her strange husband, the Bullocks and the Peters, the lone woman and her children, the man who had taken the woman and child out to Plataea on the pedallo, the woman and her young lover, the two old women from The Delphi.

They fall away into a dark background, and he thinks of Mrs Person, and the Elgin Marbles.

Someone raises a glass. 'Andreas!'

The toast is for him. But they are warm-hearted, these people, and he likes them. He remembers that when the Germans had overrun the country it was the British who had stood firm in Syntagma Square. They are a mad race. And he likes them for their money. He counts the heads around the table, and counts them in thousands of drachmas. Thousands and thousands of drachmas. He'll teach that bastard Elgin.

'Your health,' he responds, and smiles at the headmaster, and he drinks, but slowly. In time he recognises that the Mosses are missing, and as he does so Christos, his cousin, comes up to the table and tells him the deflated remnants of a plastic dinghy have just been hauled in by one of Vangelis' cousins while out fishing for octopus. Andreas nods, and abruptly leaves the table.

Sarah Greenbaum watches Christos as he walks up the beach and stops to talk to Andreas. She catches urgency in the man's face as he gesticulates, turns and points to the sea. She watches Andreas' face and notices one hand move nervously up from the table to hover hesitantly around his chin. 'Something's happened,' she whispers to her husband.

Mo feels a light body move against his legs. He kicks out and a kitten flies out from the other side of the table. Sarah watches the two Greeks walks away. 'I can feel it,' she says. 'Damn cats,' Mo mutters. 'Bloody things have probably got rabies. I'd shoot the lot of them.'

George Moore grins as another kitten scrambles up on Mo's left side, jumping up on his arm and then on to the table. Seconds later it too lands screaming on the beach on the far side of the table. Mo Greenbaum stands, one hand propped on the table, eyes wild. Sarah comes up to him and reaches out her hand for his arm. 'I told you to take your pills,' she says quietly. 'Look at the state of you. You nearly killed the poor thing.'

'I meant to,' he says firmly. He sits down again and reaches for the retsina. 'Did you write your article?' Maeve asks him. 'As a matter of fact, yes I did,' he replies, which surprises her. 'Oh?' 'Yes.' He grins at her. 'He's pleased with himself,' Sarah explains, leaning across to Maeve. 'Terribly pleased.'

'What's it about?' Maeve asks. He hesitates, then says, 'Cats.'

'Cats?'

'Yes.'

'But you can't write an article about cats,' she protests.

'Why not? Fellow in London made a musical about the bloody things. Made millions.'

'Yes, dear,' Sarah says, patting his head. 'You see,' she continues, explaining to Maeve, 'Mo actually hates cats. Hates them with enormous passion, don't you, dear? Especially Greek cats.

And his little article is, well, quite nice, really.'

'How is it nice?' Maeve asks her.

'Oh, it's vicious, foul invective,' Sarah says rolling her eyes. 'I think Mo wrote it as an act of revenge.' Mo eyes the two women, and swallows retsina. 'Revenge on what?' Maeve persists. 'Oh, the whole thing, I suppose. Beef tomatoes, feta cheese, moussaka and lamb souvlakis.' 'The whole bloody lot,' Mo adds. 'The bloody food and the bloody heat and all those bloody tragedies, and the endless bloody statues and amphitheatres. The whole sodding lot.'

'How crude,' Maeve observes.

'Yes, well I suppose that is one way of looking at it,' Sarah says interceding. 'But then passion is never reasonable, is it, dear?'

Mo looks up and down the table and says, 'Where are the Mosses? You know, that young couple with all the cocktails?' Sarah feels her sixth sense is trying to tell her something. It is a moment she remembers later, and will recall a hundred times in future conversations. 'Haven't you enjoyed your holiday, Mr Greenbaum?' Betty asks, genuinely concerned at the man's outburst. He smiles down the table at the two elderly women. Harriet Simmons, he notices, is in another appalling dress, a green and white summer creation intended for a woman perhaps fifty years younger.

'I have a very English stomach,' he says. 'It rejects foreign food.'

'Mo!' his wife warns him. 'Don't!'

Harriet Simmons nods vigorously in agreement with Mo. 'I had a friend once. Went to France. Or Spain. Some place like that. She took enough sandwiches for a week. Never had any problems. Got to keep them moist, mind you. Got to keep them moist.' She smiles around her.

Betty has a premonition that next year she will not be in Tiryns.

Harriet is going to die.

Betty is terrified by the impending freedom, and the inescapable poverty which is so bound to colour it, and in desperation she looks nervously about, and smiles simperingly at the men, women and children. George Moore catches the look on her face and wonders what awfulness would attach itself to deeper knowledge of these two women. He too looks on the next day, with its flight home, and the inevitable return to what so far has passed for normality, with a certain amount of dread. The holiday has affected them both. He has noticed Julia, deep in thought, alone on the beach, and he has felt alone with her in the flat. He wonders if she will leave him. The thought confuses him and he turns to Maeve and watches her pick slowly at a plate of squid. Her fingers are long and move delicately among the pink and white flesh. She concentrates on her eating, sucking the flesh from her fingers and moving it around in her mouth slowly. George watches her lips part, and her eyes light up as she catches him watching her. I want to pull your dress off, he tells her, and the words bang around inside his head, unspoken. Actually, what I want to do, is put my tongue in there with the squid. The unspoken proclamation provokes a rush of embarrassment and he reaches for the wine. Tonight is their last night. 'What did you get up to last night?' Julia asks innocently. 'Oh, I thought you knew?' Maeve says with some surprise. Julia raises an eyebrow. Maeve laughs and says, 'I was with George. We went to the cinema.'

'The cinema?' Julia's voice rises.

'Didn't he tell you?'

Julia shakes her head and decides to be quiet about her whereabouts the previous evening. She has memories of a flaming red and blue icon, of Saint Sebastian quivering under a hail of arrows, and of a large bed in a white, bare room. She flushes red. 'King Kong,' Maeve tells her. 'Not that George saw much of it. How did you get in such a state, George?'

'Drink,' he says deliberately. 'I drank too much.'

'I wish you wouldn't,' Julia observes.

'And where did you get to, darling?' George

asks his wife. Maeve turns her attention on Julia and knows that she is going to lie. 'Oh, nowhere much. I just went for a walk.'

'And?'

'And an ice cream,' she adds with a rush, and starts to laugh, a long echoing laugh that comes up from her stomach, and brings the table to total silence.

Andreas and Christos go to the apartment used by the Mosses and find the door open. The couple are not there. 'You saw them go out in the dinghy? Are you sure?' Andreas questions. Christos is quite sure. 'Something's happened,' Andreas says. He fears the worst, but does not say it. Christos asks him what he is going to do, but Andreas does not answer. He doesn't know what he is going to do.

The room is neat, well kept. The sheets on the bed are straight and tucked under the mattress at the sides. Clothes are hidden in the cupboard. Two small piles of books lie beside the bed, one on his bedside table, and one on hers. Andreas picks things up, and puts them down. A bottle of nail varnish remover. A hairdryer. A photograph of a small dog. The two men are silent, and stand helplessly in the room, uncertain what to do next

As they move for the door Andreas is arrested by writing on the mirror in the bedroom. The writing is large, scrawled, the product of red lipstick. He goes closer to the mirror and reads:

One ounce dry gin
One ounce cherry brandy
One tablespoon dry vermouth
Shake with ice, strain, and add ice.

Bet you can't remember what this one's called.
Love Elaine.

'They're alright, then,' Christos says from the doorway. 'We'll come back tomorrow,' Andreas replies, nonplussed by the message.

It is Maeve who makes the suggestion. 'Why don't we go to The Delphi for a drink?' George looks at Julia. Martin stares at Coronisi. When he gets home is going to cook himself the largest steak he can lay his hands on. He thinks of pints of real ale. He drives alone along narrow lanes. He does not want the Moores to come back to The Delphi. 'Yes, come on back,' he says. Gail says she is going to the disco. George has seen her with another young man, and is not surprised. 'Don't fall in love, for God's sake. We're going home tomorrow.'

'Ha, ha.'

'Leave her alone, George,' Julia tells him.

'Just some fatherly advice, Julia.'

'I wouldn't classify that as advice.'

George notices that Tom stands close and is unusually withdrawn. 'What is it?' he asks his son. 'Nothing.' 'What kind of nothing?' 'Nothing nothing. Dad, where are you going?'

'With Mum.'

The boy nods. 'But where?

'To The Delphi.'

Tom looks at Maeve and Martin and then says, 'With them?'

'Yes.'

'Can I come?'

George is genuinely surprised and asks why. 'Because. Because I'm not old enough for the disco and I don't have any cash, and I wanna know what you guys are doing, that's why.'

George tells him that it's just for drinks but Tom is adamant and says he doesn't care, and then appeals to his mother, begging her to let him come along. George remembers the boy crying and is mystified. 'OK,' he says. Julia interrupts and says, 'Why should he?' Typically, he is to tell himself later, George handles it badly. 'What do you think,

Maeve?' he asks. Tom is aghast, scandalised that his immediate future should be jeopardised by someone he only dimly recognises. Martin responds to the situation with pure instinct. 'When I was your age my father made sure I was in bed by this time.' He glares across the table at the young boy. Tom stares into the eyes of a grizzly bear. He sees a vast tongue rolling out between sharp fangs. He hears the bear panting. 'Yeh,' Tom says thoughtfully. 'That may be, but your dad and my dad don't see things the same way.'

They watch Andreas come down the beach and it strikes George first, and then Maeve, that there is something unspoken in the air. 'It's OK,' George says finally to his son. 'Thanks Dad.' Tom goes to his father and Julia watches as the boy puts an arm round her husband's neck.

Tom sees the bear draw back his lips.

They go to The Delphi. Martin brings down a bottle of scotch. Alexos sends out some wine, promising that it's the best in Tiryns. Julia eyes it suspiciously. 'How good does that make it?' she wonders aloud.

'Lousy,' Tom says. He sits on a chair, knees drawn up, just to one side of them. There is a light wind. The night is black. 'Shut up, Tom,' Julia says, voice riding high. 'He's probably right,'

Maeve adds. Quietly, Julia says to Maeve, 'Don't you and Martin want children?' George admires the question, and looks fondly at his wife. Martin pours two glasses of scotch. 'You girls drinking wine?'

'Do we have to?' Julia asks.

'Alexos won't like it if you don't,' Tom observes. He waits for the answer to his mother's question. But there is no answer. 'Where did you go last year?' Julia asks the other couple. The cicadas are loud and fill the silence that stretches between the slow movements of the sea. The tables outside The Delphi are almost empty; it is late. In front of them Aphrodite is as dark as the night itself. The harbour walls to the right of them are vague forms, barely visible. 'Bermuda,' Maeve tells her.

'We went to Yarmouth,' George says enthusiastically.

'No, we didn't. We didn't go anywhere,' Julia says, furious at her husband.

'Well, we wanted to go to Yarmouth.'

'No, we didn't.'

'Well, I wanted to go. Maybe I didn't tell you.'

'Do you think it's just me that does this to him?' Julia asks, turning to Maeve for help. Martin savours the scotch and becomes maudlin. He puts his arm up and it reaches for George's shoulder. George acquiesces. Julia sees their son is now asleep. He is small, curled up in the chair, quiet at last. She tells herself that she is happy. Memories of the past two weeks flash by, moving fast at first, then slowly, till at last they turn her attention back to George. She stares at her husband; she can handle George. And Lawrence Brown? What about him?

'I'm glad we met you,' Martin slurs.

George raises his glass. Julia drowns the memory of the icon, glowing red and blue and gold, in another glass of wine. 'Actually,' she says in reference to the wine, 'it's quite good.'

Much later they go swimming. The Delphi end of the beach is nearly empty, but further down towards the Villa Diana late night couples sit and talk; the murmur of their voices rises and falls like rushes of wind. But Julia is loud and joyful. 'Remember the cat?' she cries out, laughing. She and George go to stand at the water's edge and watch Martin struggle with a small army of cats that have just arrived on the beach.

'Couldn't forget it, could I?' He puts his arm round her waist.

'Who told Georgios to build the wall?' she asks.

'It was his idea.' Then Maeve joins them and says, 'What happened to the smell?' Julia wonders.

'I suppose we just got used to it. Maybe it just went. Just like that.' 'What about a swim?' Maeve says, putting a naked foot in the water. Julia coughs. 'Haven't got the right things. No swim suit.'

So?'

'Yes, why not?' George says.

'You haven't got any swimming trunks, George. They're in the villa.'

Well, it's not as though anyone's going to see us,' he tells her. 'It's pitch black. No nothing. No moon. Look at it out there. Hey!' he shouts at Martin. 'Fancy a swim?' Martin lurches towards them. 'What's the water like?'

Julia kicks off a shoe. 'Warm. It's OK.' 'We'll go there,' Maeve says, taking George's arm. 'By the harbour wall. Just hang on a second and I'll get a few towels.' Maeve disappears in the direction of the hotel, and her place is taken by Tom, who tugs at his father's arm. 'What's going on?' he demands of his father. 'Oh, nothing much.'

'But she said you were going for a swim.' He points at the hotel into which Maeve has just disappeared. 'That's right,' George agrees. 'What, with no clothes?'

'Why not?'

Tom stares at the hotel and then says logically, 'if she's gone for some towels, she could bring back her swimming suit.' George makes a bet with himself that she forgets her swimming suit. Staring at the water, Tom says, 'where?'

'Where what?'

'Where are you gonna swim?'

'Don't know. There.' George points at the harbour wall.

Tom catches breath and say, 'No. No, not there.' Mother and father stare at the boy. 'He's tired,' Julia observes. 'We should've sent him to bed.'

Why don't you swim there?' Tom says and points away from the harbour.

Maeve returns and the adults make their way to the harbour wall. In the dark they get separated and Maeve walks ahead with George. Trailing behind, unseen and forgotten, Tom relives the moments of his last dive by the harbour wall. George reaches for Maeve's hand.

'You're not a very faithful man, Mr Moore.' He draws her in close by the waist. 'I'm going to go naked into the sea with you,' she whispers.

'I'll have to imagine it all,' he says, gesturing at the moonless night.

'Aren't you worried?' she asks. 'This. Me and you?'

'Yes. No. I'm not sure.'

'If we made love?'

George has considered the possibility frequently.
'How I feel about Julia, you mean?' he asks.
'Yes.'
'OK. What about you and Martin?'
'Shh!' She stops him. They are on the far side of the harbour, on a small spit of beach. The wall reaches out to the sea on their left side. Aphrodite is invisible. 'Where are the others?' she asks. George turns and listens, and hearing nothing says, 'They've stopped. Martin probably had to sit down for a drink.' He watches Maeve undress and then walk quickly into the sea. Seconds later he joins her. They stand together in the water, and he puts his arms around her. Above them a small figure squats and stares down, hardly daring to breathe. Maeve laughs and breaks away, and George follows her. Splashing, she falls into the water. George pursues, and loses her. Tom rushes along the top of the wall, and hears his father call out the woman's name.

The sea is silent, and George stands alone. Smiling, he looks about him, and wades through the water beside the harbour wall; and then he dives. Tom peers over the edge, and seconds later sees Maeve break the surface about ten metres away. She calls out to George, but he does not hear her as he kicks and pushes to the bottom of the sea by the edge of the harbour wall. He tells himself that she's hiding, but he'll find her. She can't stay down that long. He pushes hard, his whole body warmed by a strength which is new to him. Just as he is about to come up for air his hands push into something which is familiar, but whose identity he cannot place, though as he kicks up to the surface and gasps for breath he knows that he has been touched by something which frightens him. He looks for Maeve, but she has disappeared, also in search. He goes down again, and within seconds knows that he has found the body of a woman.

When he comes to the surface it is to yell, and it is Maeve's name that he screams out.

Maeve surfaces, and Julia and Martin rush to join them. Tom squats still on the wall, rocking backwards and forwards on his heels. When the adults find him he screams at them. 'I kept trying to tell you! I kept trying to tell you!'

An hour later Elaine Moss is pulled from the sea.

FRIDAY

It's all over now. We're going home. But I could never have imagined an end like this. A large group of us have spent the day in The Ship. I thought when it began to happen, when the Greebaums came in, and then the Bullocks, and Ann Preston, that it would be awful, that we would sit and rummage around with feelings of guilt and inadequacy. But it hasn't been that way. Instead there has been a constant edge of excitement, people talking as though long old friends.

So, Elaine Moss is dead, and her husband is missing. I've whispered that to myself a hundred times today but it just seems to have no effect. I can't feel any sorrow, or grief. I think it's been the same for all of us.

When George yelled from the sea last night Martin started running, and I followed. George was standing in shallow water with Maeve near by, as amazed and confused as we were. 'What in the hell...?' Martin cried out. He was blowing so hard I thought he'd keel over. 'It's a body,' George said at last, his voice shaking, almost, I thought, close to laughter.

'George!' I warned him. He sloshed out of the water and stood on the beach, stark naked. I think

Martin was even more surprised than I was. 'For God's sake, George!' he yelled out, and then fell silent as Maeve came out, breasts high, naked as Venus. We both stared at them, unable to explain to ourselves what was going on.

But it was Maeve who surprised us by saying, 'What happened?' She grabbed a towel and threw it round herself.

'I was looking for you,' George told her. He suddenly became aware that he was naked and went to get a towel.

'That was what I was doing,' Maeve said. And then in a rush George said that he had found the body of a woman, and that he thought it had been Maeve.

The police came. It was Andreas who went in to get the body. He brought the girl out in his arms; no one said a thing as they watched, not a word. The police told us to go home; Andreas insisted.

George and I left Martin and Maeve and walked home. Tom told us how he'd found the body in the afternoon, and he, at least, slept. George and I lay on our backs and drifted in and out of sleep, till Gail came in from the disco. And then for an hour or two we all slept.

Harriet Simmons started trouble by telling Alexos at The Delphi what she and Betty had seen through their binoculars. The police interviewed them at length, and from what we could gather the two old women loved every second of it. At eleven o'clock police reinforcements came in from Nafplion, and went out to Aphrodite in two boats. The young men had left, of course. Disappeared. Apparently, apart from a few piles of ash and partly burnt wood there was hardly any sign they'd ever been there.

Throughout the day rumour passed backwards and forwards. We packed up and hauled our suitcases up to the offices of Minoa Travel, where the bus for the airport is going to pick us up at ten in the evening. It is now nine o'clock. In an hour we will pile into the bus and drive for three and a half hours to Athens. The bus will be hot and airless and I'm going to hate it. I've spent most of the day sitting in the corner of The Ship. My notebook is in front of me. George watches. He has never asked me about my noteboooks. Ever.

TEN

Jo Bullock sits in the corner of The Ship next to his wife and watches Julia Moore writing in her diary. The news of Elaine Moss's death has not surprised him. It is in a way almost a logical consequence of having those three young men so close for such a long time. 'We should have expected it,' he says to Martin. 'Yes, but we don't know what happened, do we?' Martin says cautiously.

'Of course we do. That woman, Harriet Simmons, saw them, didn't she?'

'God knows what she saw,' Martin says quietly. 'I'm damned if she does.' In an hour they will be on the bus. The thought of it horrifies him. The airlessness. The ridiculous last bursts of camaraderie. He looks away from Jo Bullock towards the bar, where Maeve stands talking to Ann Preston. He knows that George is around, but cannot see him. 'Both of the old girls saw what those lads were up to,' Jo Bullock says stridently. 'Both of them.'

'Anyway,' Martin says. 'We don't know what the coroner's report will say. They haven't found the other body, and the young men, if it was them, have cleared off. And,' he adds, 'if they do catch them and there is a trial, our two lady friends will have to come back as witnesses.' In a nearby seat Mo Greenbaum says, 'Hadn't thought of that. Christ, imagine having to come back out to Athens.'

'Well, I don't expect they've thought much about that either,' Martin says cheerfully. 'They might have sung a different song.' He gets up and goes across to Maeve at the bar. Jo Bullock tells himself that he's glad it's all over. Mary hasn't been herself; maybe it was the sun, or the food. This morning he had had it all worked out and had explained it to her. Things get out of hand in the heat, he had told her, always had done, just as it used to happen in India and those other places when the British had been there. 'And anyway, the Greek was uneducated,' he'd added.

Mary's silence had reassured him.

His mind now turns to the coins hidden in his suitcase, nearly a dozen of them. It's a treasure trove, one that he will have for ever. 'I shall miss old Kostas,' he confides to his wife. 'He gave me something. Precious.' What he doesn't know is that Vassilis has told her all about Kostas' coins, and told her too how her husband had gone with Kostas in the boat to old Assini. Now, she listens to the story again.

She cries, but her eyes are hard and dry, and her

silence is an echo of her children's.

Martin leaves the bar, and when he comes back it is with Andreas. 'I can't take that bus,' he says to Maeve and George.
'What do you mean?' Julia asks, coming up to where they are standing at the bar. Andreas stands next to them, agitated. The drowned body of the young woman has haunted him all day. 'So Andreas got us a taxi,' Martin continues. 'Yes, but we can't all get in the taxi,' Maeve points out.
'You and Maeve take the taxi, Martin,' Julia says, alarmed by the expense. 'We'll go by bus as planned.' 'No, you and George go by taxi,' Maeve says to Martin. I'll stay with Julia. Martin will pay,' she adds. This is followed by moments of confusion and protest but Maeve insists, and George wonders at the arrangement.
'Last round?' he suggests.
Dimitris comes across and says, 'Wait. I'll make it. How many? Four, OK?'
'What is it?' Maeve asks, as she watches Dimitris preparing his special cocktail. Dimitris looks back over his shoulder and says, 'Dry gin, cherry brandy, dry vermouth, and a little ice.'
'What's it called?' Julia asks.
Andreas stands by the bar and remembers the

writing on the mirror in the Moss's flat. He stands quite still; his eyes are tired, his face drawn. He listens to the questions and wonders why Dimitris takes so long to answer. As he stares at the drinks being made up, one by one, he sees the lipstick moving across the glass of the mirror, the fingers white, the hand in shadow.

'Kiss In The Dark,' Dimitris says finally. 'Elaine told me about it.'

The bus fills and departs. It does so quickly, and the leaving is almost painless. Stavros has elected not to come and say goodbye. Besides, he has met a girl from London, called Karen. In the end, after the suitcases and beach umbrellas and rolled mats are packed away into the hold of the bus it is only Andreas who stands there to say goodbye. The men, women, and children scuttle aboard, ghosts that he can hardly remember. Louise is the last to board the bus. She does so cheerily, and Andreas knows that the end has finally come when she calls out, 'Hi, everybody! What, lost your tongues? Let's try again. Hi, everybody!'

Some say 'Hi,' and the bus leaves.

Andreas watches the space left by the bus. He thinks suddenly of the three young men, and knows that they are gone forever, they will never be caught, there will be no trial. And he knows too that the old women will die, and that one day, next year, or the year after, some of these men and women will return.

Then the taxi gets ready to leave, and Andreas shakes hands with the two men. 'Do you still feel such a good European?' he asks Martin.

'Come back next year,' he says to George, but he knows that he will never see the headmaster again.

Andreas speaks rapidly in Greek to the driver. 'OK,' he says to them in English, 'you have a special price to the airport.' And then the taxi pulls away. Both George and Martin turn and look behind them as the taxi climbs away from Tiryns. From the taxi the bay looks dark and still, except for Coronisi, once again lit up by floodlights. 'It must be strange in winter,' Martin says.

'Coming back to see?' George asks him. Martin shakes his head. And then, seriously, George says, 'Martin, I want you to know that we didn't do anything, I mean, Maeve and me. Nothing happened.'

Martin nods. 'I know. It never does.'

'What do you mean?'

'I know her,' Martin says with some finality. Then adds, 'She has bad dreams. Nightmares.'

'What about?'

Martin does not answer, and George continues,

'It's just that I didn't want you to worry, that's all.'
The taxi driver passes Stavros' villa, and suddenly accelerates. There is a question which Martin wants to ask George, but he finds it impossible. He wants to ask the headmaster if this lack of success with Maeve makes him in any way a good man. Martin struggles with the task of asking the question and finally gives up, telling himself that he would probably not know how to handle the answer.

The orange groves are dark as they pass the great mass of old Assini, and through the open window they hear the single howl of a dog among the ruins.

Back in Tiryns the Villa Diana stands empty. The taverna next door has only a few customers. A lone bouzouki strikes up in the corner.

On the beach a cats sits and stares at the water.